CHRONICLES ABROAD

Berlin

CHRONICLES ABROAD

Berlin

EDITED BY JOHN MILLER

AND TIM SMITH

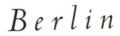

CHRONICLE BOOKS

SAN FRANCISCO

Printed in Singapore.
Page 210-11 constitutes a continuation of the copyright page.

Library of Congress Cataloging-in-Publication Data available.
ISBN 0-8118-1081-X

Editing and design: Big Fish Books
Composition: Jennifer Petersen, Big Fish Books

Distributed in Canada by Raincoast Books,
8680 Cambie Street, Vancouver, B.C. V6P 6M9

10 9 8 7 6 5 4 3 2 1

Chronicle Books
275 Fifth Street
San Francisco, CA 94103

Once again, thanks to Maggie dePagter

Contents

Vladimir Nabokov

PREFACE

WE SHALL GO still further back, to a morning in May
1934, and plot with respect to this fixed point the graph of a
section of Berlin. There I was walking home, at 5 A.M., from
the maternity hospital near Bayerischer Platz, to which I had
taken you a couple of hours earlier. Spring flowers adorned
the portraits of Hindenburg and Hitler in the window of a
shop that sold frames and colored photographs. Leftist
groups of sparrows were holding loud morning sessions in
lilacs and limes. A limpid dawn had completely unsheathed

Vladimir Nabokov was one of the greatest prose writers of the twentieth century.
He lived in Berlin from 1923-1937; in this autobiographical passage he
describes the dawn following the birth of his son.

one side of the empty street. On the other side, the houses still looked blue with cold, and various long shadows were gradually being telescoped, in the matter-of-fact manner young day has when taking over from night in a well-groomed, well-watered city, where the tang of tarred pavements underlies the sappy smells of shade trees; but to me the optical part of the business seemed quite new, like some unusual way of laying the table, because I had never seen that particular street at daybreak before, although, on the other hand, I had often passed there, childless, on sunny evenings.

In the purity and vacuity of the less familiar hour, the shadows were on the wrong side of the street, investing it with a sense of not inelegant inversion, as when one sees reflected in the mirror of a barbershop the window toward which the melancholy barber, while stropping his razor, turns his gaze (as they all do at such times), and, framed in that reflected window, a stretch of sidewalk shunting a procession of unconcerned pedestrians in the wrong direction, into an abstract world that all at once stops being droll and loosens a torrent of terror.

Bertolt Brecht

THE JOB

or

BY THE SWEAT OF THY BROW SHALT THOU FAIL TO EARN THY BREAD

IN THE DECADES after the Great War unemployment and the oppression of the lower orders went from bad to worse. An incident which took place in Mainz shows better than any peace treaty, history book or statistical table the barbaric condition to which the great European countries had been reduced by their inability to keep their economies going except by force and exploitation. One day in 1927, a poverty-stricken

---

Bertolt Brecht is primarily known for the innovative drama The Threepenny Opera. *This rare piece of fiction, "The Job," characterizes the economic crisis during the decline of the Weimar Republic. Brecht died in Berlin in 1956.*

family in Breslau called Hausmann, consisting of husband, wife and two small children, received a letter from a former workmate of Hausmann's offering him his job, a position of trust which he was giving up because of a small legacy in Brooklyn. The letter caused feverish excitement in the family which three years of unemployment had brought to the verge of desperation. The man (who was down with pneumonia) rose at once from his sick-bed, asked his wife to put a few essentials in his old case and several cardboard boxes, took his children by the hand, told his wife how she was to close down their miserable home, and in spite of his weakened condition, went to the station. (He hoped that, whatever happened, taking the children with him would confront his friend with a fait accompli.) Slumped in his compartment with a high fever, he was glad to let a young fellow traveller, a housemaid who had been sacked and was on her way to Berlin, take care of his children, supposing him to be a widower. She even bought them a few little things that she paid for out of her own money. In Berlin his condition was so bad that he had to be taken almost unconscious to hospital. There he died five hours later. The housemaid, a certain Fraülein Leidner, had not foreseen this eventuality, so she had not left the children but taken them with her to her cheap lodgings. She had paid all sorts of expenses for the dead man and his children, and she was sorry for the helpless little mites, so, without due consideration perhaps, for it would doubtless have been better to send word to Frau Hausmann, asking her to come, she went back to Breslau the same evening with the children. Frau Hausmann took the news with the terrible blank placidity that you sometimes find in people who have long forgotten what a peaceful, normal existence is like. For the whole of the next day the two women were busy buying cheap mourning clothes on hire-purchase. Meanwhile they set about clearing out the house, though this now of course made no sense at all. Standing in the empty rooms, laden with cases and card-board boxes, the woman was struck just before their departure by a terrible thought. The job which was lost when she lost her husband had not been out of her mind for a minute. The only thing that mattered was to salvage it at all costs: Fate could not be expected to make such an offer a second time.

At the last moment she adopted a plan that was as bold as her situation was desperate: she aimed to stand in for her husband and take the job as nightwatchman—for that is what it was—disguised as a man. No sooner had she settled this in her own mind than she tore the black rags from her body, undid the cord of the suitcase, pulled out her husband's Sunday suit and clumsily put it on before her children's eyes, with the help of her new-found friend who had almost instantaneously understood what she was up to. Thus it was a new family that travelled to Mainz to renew the assault on the promised job, and one that consisted of no more mouths than before. Even so do fresh recruits fill the gaps caused by gunfire in the ranks of decimated battalions.

The date by which the current holder of the job had to join his ship in Hamburg did not permit the women to leave the train at Berlin for Hausmann's funeral. While he was being moved, unaccompanied, from the hospital to be lowered into his grave, his wife was being shown round the factory in his very clothes with his papers in her pocket by his former workmate with whom she had quickly come to an arrangement. She had spent an extra day in the workmate's flat—all this incidentally in front of the children—practising her husband's walk, his way of sitting and eating, and his manner of speech under the eyes of his workmate and her new friend. Little time elapsed between the moment when Hausmann was committed to the grave and the moment when she took the promised job.

Brought back to life—that is to say, to the process of production—by a combination of fortune and fate, the two women led their new life in the most orderly and circumspect fashion as Herr and Frau Hausmann with their children. The job of nightwatchman in a big factory is not undemanding. The nightly rounds of the yards, workshops and stores calls for reliability and courage, qualities that have from time immemorial been called *manly*. The fact that Hausmann's widow was equal to these demands—she even received a public commendation from the management for having caught and secured a thief (a poor devil who was trying to steal some wood) proves that courage, physical strength and presence of mind can be shown by anybody, man or woman, who really needs a job. In a few days the woman became a man, in the same way as men have become men over the millennia: through the production process.

For four years, the little family with its growing children lived in relative security while all around them unemployment increased. Thus far the Hausmanns' domestic situation had aroused no suspicion in the neighbourhood. But then came an incident which had to be smoothed over. The caretaker of the block often sat in the Hausmanns' flat of an evening. The three of them played cards. The "nightwatchman" sat there with legs apart, in shirtsleeves, a tankard of beer in front of her (a picture later to be given prominence in the illustrated magazines). Then the nightwatchman went on duty, leaving the caretaker sitting with the young wife. Intimacy was unavoidable. Now whether Fraülein Leidner let the cat out of the bag, or whether the caretaker saw the nightwatchman changing through a half-open door, suffice it to say that a point came when the Hausmanns began to have trouble with him. He was a drinking man whose job provided him with a free flat but not much else, and from then on they had to make payments to him. Things got particularly difficult when the neighbours began to notice Hasse's—that was his name—visits to the Hausmann flat, and Frau Hausmann's habit of taking leftovers and bottles of beer to the caretaker's office became a subject of gossip in the neighbourhood. Rumours about the nightwatchman's indifference to the indecent goings-on in his flat even reached the factory and for a time shook the management's confidence in him. The three were forced to stage a break in their friendship for public consumption. Of course, however, the caretaker's exploitation of the two women did not stop, but got even worse. An accident at the factory put an end to the whole thing and brought the catastrophic affair to a conclusion.

When one of the boilers blew up one night, the nightwatchman was injured, not seriously, but badly enough to be carried away unconscious. When Frau Hausmann woke up, she found herself in a hospital for women. She was unspeakably outraged. With wounds in her legs and back, swathed in bandages, racked by nausea, but gripped by a fear even greater than could be caused by wounds whose full extent she did not know, she dragged herself through a ward full of sleeping women patients to the head nurse. Before the nurse could say a word—she was still dressing and, grotesque as it may seem, the spurious night-watchman had to overcome her acquired embarrassment at seeing a partially dressed woman, something only permitted to members of the same sex—Frau Hausmann overwhelmed her with pleas not to report the disastrous state of affairs to the management. It was not without pity that the sister told the desperate woman, who twice fainted but insisted on going on with the interview, that the papers had already gone to the factory. What she did not tell her was that the incredible story had also gone through the town like a brushfire.

The hospital released Frau Hausmann in men's clothes. She came home in the morning, and from noon on the whole quarter gathered in the hall and on the pavement outside to wait for the male impersonator. That evening the police took the unfortunate woman into custody to put an end to the uproar. She was still in men's clothes when she got into the car. She no longer had anything else.

She continued to fight for her job while in custody, needless to say without success. It was given to one of the countless thousands waiting for any vacancy, one whose legs chanced to have between them the organ recorded on his birth certificate. Frau Hausmann, who cannot be accused of leaving any stone unturned, is thought to have worked as a waitress in a suburban bar, amid photographs (some of which she had posed for *after* being found out) showing her in shirtsleeves playing cards and drinking beer as a nightwatchman and to have been regarded as resident freak by the skittle players. Thereafter she probably sank without a trace into the ranks of that army of millions who are forced to earn their modest bread by selling themselves, wholly, in part, or to one another, shedding in a few days century-old habits which had almost seemed eternal and, as we have seen, even changing sex, generally without success—who are in short lost and, if we are to believe the prevailing view, lost forever.

Marie Vassiltchikov

THE BERLIN DIARIES

TUESDAY, 23 NOVEMBER Last night the greater part of
central Berlin was destroyed.

In the afternoon there was heavy rain. I had been sent
out to fetch a document that was needed for the conference.
Our new boss Büttner has a mania for such conferences; they
take place almost daily. He probably just likes to "review his
troops." I find them a complete waste of time. I got drenched
on the way and arrived late at the meeting, which went on

The daughter of aristocratic Russian émigrés, Marie Vassiltchikov's The Berlin
Diaries 1940-1945 *offers not only an insider's perspective into the famous
July 20 plot to murder Hitler, it also reveals a woman of depth and courage.
Vassiltchikov survived the war, dying in 1978 at age 61.*

until shortly after 7 P.M. I was rushing down the stairs to go home when the hall porter intercepted me with the ominous words "Luftgefahr 15" ["air-raid danger 15"]. This meant that large enemy air formations were on their way. I took the stairs back two at a time to warn those of my colleagues who lived far away to stay put, since they might otherwise be caught out in the open. The sirens sounded just as I was leaving the building. It was still raining hard and since the buses would be stopping shortly, I decided to walk home. On the way I popped a long letter I had just written to Tatiana into the mail box on the corner.

The streets were full of people. Many just stood around, for the visibility was so poor on account of the rain that nobody expected the raid to last long or cause much damage. At home I was met by Maria Gersdorff, who told me that her husband Heinz had just telephoned from his office at the Stadt-Kommandantur [H.Q. of Berlin's garrison] to warn her that the enemy air formations were larger than usual, that the raid might therefore be serious and that he was staying on at the office for the night. Having had no time for lunch, I was ravenous. Maria asked old Martha the cook to warm up some soup while I went upstairs to change into slacks and a sweater. As one does now in such cases, I also packed a few things into a small suitcase. Papa was in his room, giving a language lesson to two young men. He told me that he did not wish to be disturbed.

I had just finished packing when the *flak* opened up. It was immediately very violent. Papa emerged with his pupils and we all hurried down to the half-basement behind the kitchen, where we usually sit out air-raids. We had hardly got there when we heard the first approaching planes. They flew very low and the barking of the *flak* was suddenly drowned by a very different sound—that of exploding bombs, first far away and then closer and closer, until it seemed as if they were falling literally on top of us. At every crash the house shook. The air pressure was dreadful and the noise deafening. For the first time I understood what the expression *Bombenteppich* ["bomb carpet"] means—the Allies call it "saturation" bombing. At one point there was a shower of broken glass and all three doors of the basement flew into the room, torn off their hinges. We pressed them back into place and leaned against them to try to keep them shut. I had left my coat outside but didn't dare go out to get it. An incendiary flare fell hissing into our entrance and the men crept out to extinguish it. Suddenly we realised that we had no water on hand to put out a possible fire and hastily opened all the taps in the kitchen. This dampened the noise for a few minutes, but not for long . . . The planes did not come in waves, as they do usually, but kept on droning ceaselessly overhead for more than an hour.

In the middle of it all the cook produced my soup. I thought that if I ate it I would throw up. I found it even impossible to sit quietly and kept jumping to my feet at every crash. Papa, imperturbable as always, remained seated in a wicker armchair throughout. Once, when I leapt up after a particularly deafening explosion, he calmly remarked: "Sit down! That way, if the ceiling collapses you will be farther away from it . . ." But the crashes followed one another so closely and were so earsplitting that at the worst moments I stood behind him, holding on to his shoulders by way of self-protection. What a family *bouillabaisse* we would have made! His pupils cowered in a corner, while Maria stood propped against a wall, praying for her husband and looking desperate. She kept advising me to keep away from furniture, as it might splinter. The bombs continued to rain down and when a house next to ours collapsed, Papa muttered in Russian: "Volia Bozhia!" ["Let God's will be done!"]. It seemed indeed as if nothing could save us. After an hour or so it became quieter, Papa produced a bottle of schnapps and we all took large gulps. But then it started all over again . . . Only around 9:30 P.M. did the droning of planes overhead cease. There must have been several hundreds of them.

Just then, marvel of marvels, the kitchen telephone rang. It was Gottfried Bismarck, from Potsdam, enquiring whether we were all right. They had heard hundreds of planes flying very low over their heads, but because of the poor visibility they could not tell how much damage had been done. When I said: "It was awful!" he volunteered to come over and fetch me, but I told him that it was not worth it, as the worst seemed over. He promised to find out where Loremarie Schönburg was and ring back.

The all-clear came only half an hour after the last planes had departed, but long before that we were called out of the house by an unknown naval officer. The wind, he told us, thus far non-existent, had suddenly risen and the fires, therefore, were spreading. We all went out into our little square and, sure enough, the sky on three sides was blood-red. This, the officer explained, was only the beginning; the greatest danger would come in a few hours' time, when the fire storm really got going. Maria had given each of us a wet towel with which to smother our faces before leaving the house—a wise precaution, for our square was already filled with smoke and one could hardly breathe.

We went back into the house and Papa's pupils climbed up on the roof to keep an eye on the surrounding fires. Then the Danish chargé d'affaires Steenson (who lives next door) appeared, hugging a bottle of brandy. While we stood in the drawing-room, talking and taking an occasional gulp, the telephone rang once more. It was again Gottfried and he sounded desperately worried. He had called up Berndt Mumm's flat, where Loremarie had been dining with Aga Fürstenberg, only to be told that Loremarie had disappeared immediately after the all-clear and no one knew where she had gone. Gottfried thought that she might be trying to rejoin me, but as we were inside a ring of fire, I doubted whether she would get through.

Strangely, as soon as he hung up our telephone broke down; that is, people could still call *us,* but *we* could not get through to anyone. Also the electricity, gas and water no longer worked and we had to grope our way around with electric torches and candles. Luckily we had had time to fill every available bath tub, wash basin, kitchen sink and pail. By now the wind had increased alarmingly, roaring like a gale at sea. When we looked out of the window we could see a steady shower of sparks raining down on our and the neighbouring houses and all the time the air was getting thicker and hotter, while the smoke billowed in through the gaping window frames. We went through the house and found to our relief that apart from the broken windows and the unhinged doors, it had not suffered any real damage.

Just as we were swallowing some sandwiches, the sirens came on once more. We stood at the windows for about half an hour, in total silence. We were convinced it would start all over again. Then the all-clear sounded again. Apparently enemy reconnaissance planes had been surveying the damage. Maria, who had until then been a brick, now burst into tears, for her husband had given her as yet no sign of life. Though by now I was terribly sleepy, we decided that I would keep vigil near the phone. Putting it on the floor near me, I rolled myself up in a blanket on the sofa. About I A.M. Gottfried and Loremarie called from Potsdam. We were cut off almost immediately, but at least we were spared further anxiety on her account.

Towards 2 A.M. I decided to sleep for a while. Papa came and held his torch over me as I took off my shoes and tried to wash. Towards three, Maria also lay down. Presently I heard the telephone ring and then her ecstatic "Liebling!", which meant that Heinz was all right. Soon she, too, fell asleep. Every now and then a crashing building or a delayed time bomb would tear one awake and I would sit up with a pounding heart. By now the fire storm had reached its peak and the roar outside was like a train going through a tunnel.

WEDNESDAY, 24 NOVEMBER Early this morning I overheard Maria Gersdorff talking anxiously to Papa. A house
nearby had caught fire. But I was so tired that I dozed off
again and staggered up only around 8 A.M.

By then, Papa's pupils had gone home after spending
the night on our roof and Maria had gone out to buy some
bread. She soon returned with an old lady on her arm,
wrapped in a white shawl. She had stumbled into her at the
street corner and, peering into her grimy face, had recognised
her own eighty-year-old mother, who had been trying to reach
her, walking through the burning town all night. Her own flat
had been completely burnt out, the firemen having arrived late
and concentrated their efforts on saving a hospital nearby
(which, thank God, they had done); but all the other houses in
the street had been destroyed. Soon Heinz Gersdorff himself
appeared. He said that as he had come straight home, he had
had only a bird's-eye view of the effects of the raid but, as far
as he could judge, the Unter den Linden area (where his office
is located) had suffered just as badly as our neighbourhood:
the French and British Embassies, the Hotel Bristol, the

Zeughaus [Arsenal] and the Wilhemstrasse and Friedrich-strasse were all very badly damaged.

Towards 11 A.M. I decided to go out and try and reach my office, in the hope—wildly optimistic, as it turned out—of jumping into a hot bath as soon as I got there. Clad in slacks, my head muffled in a scarf and wearing a pair of Heinz's fur-lined military goggles, I started off. The instant I left the house I was enveloped in smoke and ashes rained down on my head. I could breathe only by holding a handkerchief to my mouth and blessed Heinz for lending me those goggles.

At first our Woyrschstrasse did not look too bad; but one block away, at the corner of Lützowstrasse all the houses were burnt out. As I continued down Lützowstrasse the devastation grew worse; many buildings were still burning and I had to keep to the middle of the street, which was difficult on account of the numerous wrecked trams. There were many people in the streets, most of them muffled in scarves and coughing, as they threaded their way gingerly through the piles of fallen masonry. At the end of Lützowstrasse, about four blocks away from the office, the houses on both sides of the street had collapsed and I had to climb over mounds of smoking rubble, leaking water pipes and other wreckage to get across to the other side. Until then I had seen very few firemen around, but here some were busily trying to extricate people trapped in the cellars. On Lützowplatz all the houses were burnt out. The bridge over the river Spree was undamaged, but on the other side all the buildings had been destroyed, only their outside walls still stood. Many cars were weaving their way cautiously through the ruins, blowing their horns wildly. A woman seized my arms and yelled that one of the walls was tottering and we both started to run. I caught sight of the mail box into which I had dropped that long letter to Tatiana the night before; it still stood but was completely crumpled. Then I saw my food shop Krause, or rather what remained of it. Maria had begged me to buy some provisions on the way home, as the one in which her coupons were registered had been destroyed. But poor Krause would be of no help either now. [*The German food-rationing system required one to register one's coupons in a given shop from where alone rations could be drawn.*]

Somehow I could still not imagine that our office too was gone, but on reaching the corner I saw that the porter's lodge and the fine marble entrance were burning merrily. In front of it stood Strempel (a high official of the A.A.) and the Rumanian Counsellor Valeanu, surrounded by a small batch of the latter's swarthy compatriots. Valeanu threw himself on my neck, exclaiming: "Tout a péri, aussi l'appartement des jumelles! J'emmène mon petit troupeau à la campagne, à Buckow!" For all foreign missions now have emergency quarters outside of town. And true enough, the Rumanian mission further down the street, together with that of the Finns, was a smouldering ruin. I asked Stempel what we should do. He growled: "Didn't you have any contingency orders?" "Certainly," I answered sweetly. "We were quote not to panic and to assemble at the Siegessäule, [the Victory Column halfway down the Ost-West Axe], where we would be picked up by lorries and taken out of town unquote!" He shrugged his shoulders angrily and turned his back to me. I decided to go home.

By now the sight of those endless rows of burnt-out or still burning buildings had got the better of me and I was beginning to feel panicky. The whole district, many of its houses so familiar to me, had been wiped out in just one night! I started to run and kept on running until I was back in Lützowstrasse, where a building collapsed as I passed. A fireman shouted something unintelligible at me and some people close by: we all flung ourselves to the ground, I hid my head under my arms, and when the rumble and clatter of yet another collapsing wall ceased we were covered with mortar and dust, I looked up across a puddle into the smudged Japanese face of Count C.-K. Although Tatiana and I had been studiously cutting him for the last four years (he has a soft spot for pretty girls and does not always behave), I said to myself that in times like these all men are brothers and, trying a friendly smile, I exclaimed in English: "Hullo!" He eyed me coldly and enquired: "Kennen wir uns?" ["Have we met?"]. I decided that this was not the time for formal introductions and, scrambling back to my feet, hurried on.

When I got home I found some hot soup waiting. Papa took my goggles and went out to have a look in his turn. Then Gottfried Bismarck rang up and said that he would pick me up at 3 P.M. I told him which streets to take so as not to get stuck. Maria's sister, Countess Schulenburg (who is married to a cousin of the Ambassador), turned up on her bicycle. She lives at the other end of the town, which, apparently, has suffered only slight damage. That very morning three workmen had arrived at her house to replace the window panes that had been smashed during a raid in August and although all central Berlin lost its windows last night, they repaired hers.

The only material loss I have as yet sustained is my monthly ration of Harz cheese; I had bought it yesterday, and as it smelt vile and looked equally so, I had stored it outside on the window sill; in the morning it had vanished, probably blasted by the air pressure onto a neighbouring roof.

When Papa returned I took the goggles and walked over to our other office in the Kurfürstenstrasse. The ex-Polish Consulate on the corner, where Tatiana, Luisa Welczeck and I had all worked together for a long time, was burning brightly, but the Embassy building next door seemed undamaged. I took a flying leap past the former and dived into the latter's entrance, where a sorry little bunch of people had collected. Seated on the stairs were Adam Trott and Leipoldt, both with sooty faces. They had been there all night, as the raid had caught them still at work. As nothing seemed to be happening, we agreed to meet there again the following morning at eleven.

At 3 P.M. on the dot Gottfried appeared with his car. We piled my luggage into the back, together with some blankets and a pillow. As his house in Potsdam was crammed with other bombed-out friends, he explained, we would have to camp. In addition to Loremarie Schönburg, there are the Essens, who also turned up in the middle of the night, wet, bedraggled and exhausted.

Rudger Essen had been in his office just down the street from our office when the raid started; Hermine was at home (she is expecting a baby soon). He telephoned her to hurry over to the Legation, beneath which some Swedish workmen had just built a solid-concrete bunker with walls 2.5m thick. Until last night none of the diplomatic missions and homes had suffered any damage and they probably imagined that their immunity extended to bombing too! Hermine reached the bunker safely and, after the all-clear, they emerged only to find the Legation burning like a torch. They spend several hours salvaging the most precious archives and then, jumping into their car, headed for home. That, too, was now past saving, whereupon they got back into the car and drove through the burning city straight out to the Bismarcks' in Potsdam.

After picking up Rudger, we drove to the still smouldering Swedish Legation to collect some of his surviving belongings there. While Rudger was inside, Gottfried and I got out of the car to re-arrange the luggage. Just then, tottering towards us wrapped in an expensive fur coat, I saw Ursula Hohenlohe, a famous Berlin belle. Her hair was straggly, her make-up was running. She stopped before us, sobbing: "I have lost everything. *Everything!*" She was trying to reach some Spanish friends who had promised to drive her out to the country. We told her that the Spanish Embassy, too, had been destroyed. She turned away without a word and staggered off towards the smoking Tiergarten. A big piece of fur was torn out of the back of her coat.

Soon Rudger re-appeared and we threaded our way up Budapesterstrasse between straggling lines of people tugging along babies' prams, mattresses, odd bits of furniture, etc. Brandl's, Tatiana's favourite antique shop, was still burning; the flames licked at the curtains in the windows and curled around the crystal candelabra inside. As most of the materials in the shop were silks and brocades, the pink glow looked very festive, indeed sumptuous. The whole Budapesterstrasse was gutted, with the exception of the Hotel Eden, so we picked that as our meeting place in town next day. We then turned down the Ost-West Achse. We could barely believe our eyes: not a single house on either side had survived.

When we reached Potsdam the contact with the fresh, cold air at first made me dizzy. At the "Regierung," the Bismarcks' official residence, Gottfried's wife Melanie was bustling around, busily making up beds. Hermine Essen was sitting up in hers, her hair freshly washed and stiff as a little girl's. I took a bath too, Loremarie scrubbing me; the water turned black! Melanie is quite disgusted with the soot and dirt which every new arrival brings into their hitherto spotless home.

We had just finished supper when the call we had put through to Tatiana in Königswart came through and we were able to reassure her and Mamma; they had been trying all day to contact us—without success. Immediately after, Gottfried was informed that large enemy air formations were once more heading for Berlin. I rang up the Gersdorffs and Papa to warn them. I felt bad about breaking such bad news to them when I myself was safe, but at least it gave them time to dress. And sure enough a little later the sirens sounded. The others stayed in the sitting-room but Loremarie and I, still shaken by the events of the past night, went up to Jean-George's room to keep watch. The planes came flying over Potsdam in wave after wave but this time they headed farther west, towards Spandau, and so we worried less. The raid lasted about an hour, after which we collapsed into bed.

TUESDAY, 27 JUNE This time our train was on time. But half an hour before reaching Berlin it stopped in the middle of cornfields, as a heavy air-raid had just been announced. Hundreds of planes could soon be seen flying overhead—a most disagreeable sensation, as they could easily have dropped some of their load on us. Everybody became very silent and we all seemed to have lost our colour. Air attacks on trains are among the worse; one feels so totally exposed, trapped and helpless. Paul Metternich alone seemed unconcerned. At first everybody hung out of the windows until an angry old gentleman shouted that "they" would aim at all those uplifted faces shining in the sun. At which a young girl answered "Erst recht, wenn sie Ihre Glatze schen!" ["particularly when they catch sight of your bald pate!"]. We were soon ordered to scatter in the fields. Tatiana, Paul and I sat in a ditch in the middle of the corn. From where we were, we could hear the bombs falling on the city and see the smoke and explosions. Six hours later, our train started off again but even then we had to circle Berlin and debarked in Potsdam. *Adieu* once more to my meeting, assuming it was ever held.

We walked over to the Palast Hotel, where Gottfried Bismarck had reserved rooms for us, his house being full. Potsdam itself had not been hit but the whole town was covered with dense yellow smoke from the fires in Berlin.

We washed and changed and then took the S-Bahn into Berlin. I proceeded straight to the office, while the others went over to the Gersdorffs'. As luck would have it, or rather to the contrary, Dr Six was still there and Judgie

Richter, who, he says, is getting grey hair because of me, sent me in to him at once.

I assured him that the train really had been derailed but today's holocaust seemed to have softened him, for he was civil. In general, I understand that he rants about me in my absence but to my face he is always polite. Adam Trott hates him with a cold hatred and tells me that however amiable he may try to be, we must never forget what he represents. Six, for his part, seems grudgingly to realise what an extraordinary man Adam is and to be somehow fascinated by him and even to fear him. For Adam is perhaps the only man left in his entourage who is never afraid to speak up. He treats Six with infinite condescension and, curiously, the other one takes it.

At 1 A.M. that night another raid. I hurried Tatiana and Paul a little, as the shooting was already violent. At last they were dressed and we got down to the cellar, a dismal affair, rather like an old dungeon, narrow and high and full of hot-water pipes, which gave one nasty thoughts of being drenched, if hit, in boiling water. I am getting more and more nervous during air-raids. I could not even chat with Tatiana, as *Sprechen verboten* [no talking] was plastered all over the walls, probably so as not to use up oxygen should we be buried alive. Actually, I am even more frightened when Paul and Tatiana are with me than when I am alone and this is strange. Probably one's anxiety is heightened by fear for someone else. But Paul, like me, is anxious to be around just now and is always cooking up pretexts to come up to Berlin. Throughout all the noise, which was loud and frightening, he was plunged in a huge book about his ancestor, the Chancellor. After two hours we emerged.

MONDAY, 10 JULY I am back in Berlin, staying at the Adlon. Giorgio Cini is still here.

Adam Trott and I dined there together. We spoke English to the head waiter, who was delighted to show how well he still remembers it. Our neighbours began to stare. Adam then took me for a drive, during which, without going into particulars, we discussed the coming events which, he told me, are now imminent. We don't see eye to eye on this because I continue to find that too much time is being lost perfecting the details, whereas to me only one thing is really important now—the physical elimination of the man. What happens to Germany once he is dead can be seen to later. Perhaps because I am not German myself, it may all seem simpler to me, whereas for Adam it is essential that some kind of Germany be given a chance to survive. This evening we had a bitter quarrel about this and both of us got very emotional. So sad, at this, of all moments . . .

WEDNESDAY, 19 JULY Today I left Krummhübel—I suspect for good. I had packed everything and have taken with me as little as possible. The rest will stay with Madonna Blum until I know what is to happen to me.

We reached Berlin at eleven, but owing to recent air-raids all stations are in a state of chaos. Ran into old Prinz August Wilhelm, the late Kaiser's fourth son, who kindly helped carry my luggage. We finally boarded a bus. The town is enveloped in smoke; there is rubble everywhere. Eventually, I was deposited at the Gersdorffs'.

Now that it is summer, they take their meals in the upstairs sitting-room, although it still has no windows. I found the usual group of people, plus Adam Trott.

Later, I had a long talk with Adam. He looks very pale and strained, but seems glad to see me. He is appalled that Loremarie Schönburg should be back in town and is very unhappy about her unceasing efforts to bring together people whom she suspects of being sympathetic to what I call *die Konspiration* [the plot] and many of whom are already deeply involved and are having a hard enough time as it is staying above suspicion. Somehow she has found out also about Adam's involvement and now keeps pestering him and his entourage, where she has acquired the nickname "Lottchen" (after Marat's assassin, Charlotte Corday). To many she is a real security risk. He told me that she had even complained about my being unwilling to take an active part in the preparations.

The truth is that there is a fundamental difference in outlook between all of *them* and me: not being German, I am concerned only with the elimination of the Devil. I have never attached much importance to what happens afterwards. Being patriots, *they* want to save their country from complete destruction by setting up some interim government. I have never believed that even such an interim government would be acceptable to the Allies, who refuse to distinguish between "good" Germans and "bad." This, of course, is a fatal mistake on their part and we will probably all pay a heavy price for it.

We agreed not to meet again until Friday. After he had gone, Maria Gersdorff remarked: "I find he looks so pale and so tired; sometimes I think he is not going to live long."

Aga Fürstenberg joined us for supper. She has now moved to the actor Willy Fritsch's house in Grunewald, a charming little cottage he left in a hurry after having a nervous breakdown during one of the recent raids. Apparently, he lay sobbing on his bed all day until his wife came back to Berlin and took him out to the country. Aga shares the house with Georgie Pappenheim, a charming fellow who has been a diplomat for years and who has just been called back from Madrid, probably on account of his name (the Pappenheims are among the oldest families in Germany). He plays the piano beautifully.

I have been granted four weeks' sick leave but may only take two at a time and must first train an assistant to take care of things in my absence.

THURSDAY, 20 JULY This afternoon Loremarie Schönburg and I sat chatting on the office stairs when Gottfried Bismarck burst in, bright red spots on his cheeks. I had never seen him in such a state of feverish excitement. He first drew Loremarie aside, then asked me what my plans were. I told him they were uncertain but that I would really like to get out of the A.A. as soon as possible. He told me I should not worry, that in a few days everything would be settled and we would all know what was going to happen to us. Then, after asking me to come out to Potsdam with Loremarie as soon as possible, he jumped into his car and was gone.

I went back into my office and dialled Percy Frey at the Swiss Legation to cancel my dinner date with him, as I preferred to go out to Potsdam. While I waited, I turned to Loremarie, who was standing at the window, and asked her why Gottfried was in such a state. Could it be the *Konspiration?* (all that with the receiver in my hand!). She whispered: "Yes! That's it! It's done. This morning!" Just then Percy replied. Still holding the receiver, I asked: "Dead?" She answered: "Yes, dead!" I hung up, seized her by the shoulders and we went waltzing around the room. Then grabbing hold of some papers, I thrust them into the first drawer and shouting to the porter that we were *"dienstlich unterwegs"* ["off on official business"], we tore off to the Zoo station. On the way out to Potsdam she whispered to me the details and though the compartment was full, we did not even try to hide our excitement and joy:

Count Claus Schenck von Stauffenberg, a colonel on the General Staff, had put a bomb at Hitler's feet during a conference at Supreme H.Q. at Rastenburg in East Prussia. It had gone off and Adolf was dead. Stauffenberg had waited outside until the explosion and then, seeing Hitler being carried out on a stretcher covered with blood, he had run to his car, which had stood hidden somewhere, and with his A.D.C., Werner von Haeften, had driven to the local airfield and flown back to Berlin. In the general commotion nobody had noticed his escape.

On reaching Berlin, he had gone straight to the O.K.H. [Army Command H.Q.] in Bendlerstrasse, which had meanwhile been taken over by the plotters and where Gottfried Bismarck, Helldorf and many others were now gathered. (The O.K.H. lies on the other side of the canal from our Woyrschstrasse.) This evening at six an announcement would be made over the radio that Adolf was dead and that a new government had been formed. The new Reichskanzler [Chancellor of the Reich] would be Gördeler, a former mayor of Leipzig. With a socialist background, he is considered a brilliant economist. Our Count Schulenburg or Ambassador von Hassell is to be Foreign Minister. My immediate feeling was that it was perhaps a mistake to put the best brains at the head of what could only be an interim government.

By the time we had reached the Regierung in Potsdam, it was past six o'clock. I went to wash up. Loremarie hurried upstairs. Only minutes had passed when I heard dragging footsteps outside and she came in: "There has just been an announcement on the radio: "A Count Stauffenberg has attempted to murder the Führer, but Providence saved him . . ."

I took her by the arm and we raced back upstairs. We found the Bismarcks in the drawing room, Melanie with a stricken expression. Gottfried pacing up and down, up and down. I was afraid to look at him. He had just got back from the Bendlerstrasse and kept repeating: "It's just not possible! It's a trick! Stauffenberg *saw* him dead." "They" were staging a comedy and getting Hitler's double to go on with it. He went into his study to telephone Helldorf. Loremarie followed him and I was left alone with Melanie.

She started to moan: Loremarie had driven Gottfried to this; she had been working on him for years; if he were to die now, she, Melanie, was the one who would be left with three little children; maybe Loremarie could afford that luxury, but who would be left fatherless? Other children, not hers . . . It was really dreadful, and there was nothing I could say.

Gottfried came back into the room. He had not been able to get through to Helldorf, but he had further news: the main radio station had been lost; the insurgents had seized it but had been unable to make it work, and now it was back in S.S. hands. However, the officers' schools in the suburbs had taken up arms and were now marching on Berlin. And, surely enough, an hour later we heard the panzers of the Krampnitz tank training school rolling through Potsdam on their way to the capital. We hung out of the windows watching them go by and prayed. Nobody in the streets, which were practically empty, seemed to know what was going on. Gottfried kept insisting that he could not believe Hitler was unhurt, that "they" were hiding something . . .

A little later the radio announced that the Führer would address the German people at midnight. We realised that only then would we know for certain whether all this was a hoax or not. And yet Gottfried refused to give up hope. According to him, even if Hitler *was* alive, his Supreme Head-quarters in East Prussia was so far away that if things went well elsewhere, the regime could still be overthrown before he could regain control in Germany itself. But the rest of us were getting very uneasy.

Helldorf rang up several times. Also the Gauleiter of Brandenburg, asking the Potsdam Regierungspräsident Graf Bismarck what the devil he proposed to do, as he, the Gauleiter, understood that disorders and perhaps even a mutiny had broken out in the capital. Gottfried had the impudence to tell him that the orders from Supreme Headquarters were that the Führer wished all higher officials to stay put and await further instructions. In fact, he hoped that the insurgent troops would soon come and arrest the Gauleiter.

As night came, rumours began to circulate that the uprising was not succeeding as well as had been hoped. Somebody rang up from the airfield: "Die Luftwaffe macht nicht mit" ["the air force isn't going along"]; they wanted personal orders from Goering or from the Führer himself. Gottfried now began to sound sceptical—for the first time. He said such a thing had to be done fast; every minute lost was irretrievable. It was not long past midnight and still Hitler had not spoken. It all became so discouraging that I saw no purpose in sitting up any longer and went to bed. Loremarie soon followed.

At two in the morning, Gottfried looked in and in a dead voice said: "It was him all right!"

TUESDAY, 25 JULY Early today I telephoned Adam Trott at home; he was still all right. But later, when I dropped by his office, he was not there, only his secretary—a nice girl and a friend—with a scared expression on her face. Lunched in a hurry at Maria Gersdorff's and then returned to the office. This time Adam's secretary tried to shove me out of his room. I pushed past her and marched in. At his desk a small man in civilian clothes was going through his drawers. Another one lounged in an armchair. The swine! I glanced at them closer to see whether they had anything in their buttonholes, but then remembered that they wear their Gestapo badge inside. I asked the secretary ostentatiously: "Wo ist Herr von Trott? Noch immer nicht da?" ["Where is Herr von Trott? *Still* not there?"] They both looked up. When we had left the room, she looked at me beseechingly and put her finger to her lips.

I took the stairs three at a time and burst into Judgie Richter's office. I said something must be done immediately to prevent Adam from returning to his office, as the Gestapo was searching it. Judgie looked at me in a sickly way and said: "It's too late. They picked him up at noon. Luckily Alex Werth was with him and drove after them in another car, and hopefully he will soon be back with some indication why Adam has been arrested." Judgie evidently still suspects nothing. He related that Adam had attended the daily meeting at

the main A.A. office in Wilhelmstrasse. The Gestapo, meanwhile, had walked into his office and demanded to know his
whereabouts. The secretary had tried to get away to warn
him, but they had seized hold of her and had not let her leave
the room. He had walked straight into the trap. State Secretary Keppler (a high Nazi official at the A.A. who used to
head the Free India office) was expecting him for lunch in the
Adlon at one. For the moment, Dr Six seems interested in his
release; he has sent his A.D.C. to find out what the charges
were. But I doubt he will maintain this attitude.

I left the office and ran over to Maria Gersdorff.
Steenson, the Danish chargé d'affaires, was there and so I
could not say much; I merely burst into tears. Maria tried to
comfort me: it was clearly a mistake, he could not have had
much to do with it, etc. If only she knew! And yet I must not
explain anything.

A little later Heinz Gersdorff came home. He, too, is in
trouble, as his boss, the Military Commandant of Berlin, General
von Hase, whom we knew well, who had organised our visits to
Jim Viazemsky in his P.O.W. camp, and who was in the *coup* up

to his ears, has also been arrested after a stormy interview with Goebbels. Why didn't Hase shoot the rat then and there?

Several people have committed suicide, among them Count Lehndorff, on whose estate Hitler's Supreme Headquarters at Rastendorf in East Prussia is located. Prince Hardenberg shot himself in the stomach when they came to arrest him and is badly hurt. An early resister, he was under suspicion because Stauffenberg and Werner Haeften had spent their last weekend in his house. The two Gestapo men who had arrested him were killed in a motor accident on their way back to Berlin—at last a welcome piece of news! Our Hans-Bernd Haeften was arrested this morning too. It is rumoured that lists have been found.

Slept on the sofa in the Gersdorffs' living room. It still has no windows, but it is so hot that it makes no difference. At midnight, there was an air-raid and the planes were overhead so soon we scarcely had time to throw on some clothes and crawl into the cellar of the neighbouring house, which burnt down last November. They dropped mines. For the first time in years I was not afraid.

TUESDAY, 5 SEPTEMBER Tony Saurma's first day in court. The trial was immediately suspended for a fortnight while they send for further information from Silesia. Any delay these days is a good thing. But the lawyer is worried, as evidence is piling up and none of it is in Tony's favour. All seems to depend now on the decency of the judges. I wrote Tony a letter today, for I myself am leaving for Königswart tomorrow.

At the office Adam Trott's friends now believe that he *is* dead, although Tony's lawyer still thinks otherwise. But none of us can do anything either for him or Gottfried Bismarck or Count Schulenburg. Gottfried's trial too seems to have been postponed thanks to Otto Bismarck's indefatigable efforts to gain time. His name has never yet been mentioned in the press. True, a Bismarck trying to kill Hitler would not sound too good, even *they* realise that. One can only wait and pray that he will survive.

And now the time has come also for me to go. I have still some sick leave due of which I may as well take advantage. I feel relieved at going away but also depressed. We have been under such pressure these last weeks, the mind is so obsessed by all that has happened that nothing else seems to matter anymore. Also, for all the anguish, I am so accustomed now to living among these ruins, with the constant smell of gas in the air, mixed with the odour of rubble and rusty metal and sometimes even the stench of putrefying flesh, that the thought of Königswart's green fields, quiet nights and clean air actually frightens me.

At all events this seems to be the end of my Berlin life. Paul Metternich and Tatiana are meeting me in Vienna in eight days and they will no doubt talk me into staying on in Königswart until I am quite well again. I can resist family pressure from afar, but once we are all reunited I will probably agree with them.

All these weeks I had been fearing that the Allies might broadcast further particulars of the 20th July Plot (as they did in the beginning), revealing the purpose of Adam's trips abroad and thus harming him still more; but in his case they were for long mercifully discreet, starting to write about him only once the German press had announced his execution.

Das Schwarze Korps (the official S.S. paper) has been storming about "blaublütige Schweinehunde und Verräter" ["blue-blooded swine and traitors"], but a recent anonymous article in *Der Angriff* (the S.A.'s sheet) strikes, surprisingly, a contrary note: no social class in Germany, it said, had made greater sacrifices and suffered, proportionately, such heavy losses during this war as the Germany aristocracy. Some of the Nazis seem to be playing it safe.

Pütze Siemens came to lunch yesterday—she is a great friend of Maria Gersdorff's. She was in deep mourning for her brother Peter Yorck, who was hanged at the same time as Field Marshal von Witzleben. This conventional reaction to such an unconventional death seemed somehow pathetically inadequate to express such grief. She questioned me a lot about Adam, who was a friend of theirs, but we did not mention her brother. I could not have found words.

My hands are still covered with cuts from trying to open the oysters that Tony brought us just before his arrest.

VIENNA WEDNESDAY, 6 SEPTEMBER Spent my last evening in Berlin with Aga Fürstenberg and Georgie Pappenheim. Georgie escorted me home in the tram; he played a

mouth organ all the way to the enthusiasm of the other passengers. He stayed overnight, as Maria and I were alone and
wanted a man about in case of another raid. He slept in the
drawing-room on one sofa and I on another. When the old
cook, Martha, awoke me this morning, she sniffed: "In meiner
Jugend kam so etwas nicht vor, aber dieser 20. Juli stellt alles
aus den Kopf!" ("In my young days, that couldn't have happened, but this 20th July has turned everything topsy-turvy").

Alfred Döblin

BERLIN ALEXANDERPLATZ

Boom, boom, the steam pile-driver thumps in front of Aschinger's on the Alex. It's one story high, and knocks the rails into the ground as if they were nothing at all.

Icy air, February. People walk in overcoats. Whoever has a fur piece wears it, whoever hasn't, doesn't wear it. The women have on thin stockings and are freezing, of course, but they look nice. The bums have disappeared with the cold. When it gets warmer, they'll stick their noses out again. In the meantime they nip a double ration of brandy, but don't ask me what it's

Alfred Döblin's complex, Joycean vision of 1920s Berlin provides the backdrop to his famous novel, named for the working-class district where he lived for many years. He was driven from Nazi Germany in 1933.

like, nobody would want to swim in it, not even a corpse.

Boom, boom, the steam pile-driver batters away on the Alex.

A lot of people have time to spare and watch the pile-driver whacking away. Up on top there is a man who is always pulling on a chain, then there is a puff on top, and bang! the rod gets it in the neck. There they stand, men and women, especially youngsters, they love the way it works, as if it were greased, bang! the rod gets it in the neck. After that it grows small as the tip of your finger, but it gets another blow and it's welcome now to do whatever it pleases. Finally it's gone, Hell's bells, they've given it a nice drubbing, the people walk off satisfied.

Everything is covered with planks. The Berolina statue once stood in front of Tietz's, one hand outstretched, a regular giantess, now they have dragged her away. Maybe they'll melt her and make medals out of her.

People hurry over the ground like bees. They hustle and bustle around here day and night, by the hundreds.

The street-cars roll past with a screech and a scrunch, yellow ones with trailers, away they go across the planked-over

Alexanderplatz, it's dangerous to jump off. The station is laid out on a broad plan, Einbahnstrasse to Königstrasse past Wertheim's. If you want to go east, you have to pass police headquarters and turn down through Klosterstrasse. The trains rumble from the railroad station towards Jannowitz Brücke, the locomotive pulls out a plume of steam, just now it is standing above the Prälat, Schlossbräu entrance a block further down.

Across the street they are tearing down everything, all the houses along the city railroad, wonder where they get the money from, the city of Berlin is rich, and we pay the taxes.

They have torn down Loeser and Wolff with their mosaic sign, 20 yards further on they built it up again, and there's another branch over there in front of the station. Loeser and Wolff, Berlin-Elbing, A-I quality for every taste, Brazil, Havana, Mexico, Little Comforter, Lilliput, Cigar No. 8, 25 pfennigs each, Winter Ballad, package containing 25 at 20 pfennigs, Cigarillos No. 10, unselected, Sumatra wrapper, a wonderful value at this price, in boxes of a hundred, 10 pfennigs. I beat everything, you beat everything, he beats everything with boxes of 50 and cardboard packages of 10, can be mailed to every country on earth, Boyero 25 pfennigs, this novelty has won us many friends, I beat everything, but I never beat a retreat.

Alongside the Prälat there is lots of room, there are wagons standing there loaded with bananas. Give your children bananas. The banana is the cleanest of fruits, because it is protected from insects, worms, as well as bacilli, by its skin. We except such insects, worms, and bacilli as are able to penetrate the skin. Privy Councillor Czerny emphatically pointed out that even children in their first years. I beat everything to pieces, you beat everything to pieces, he beats everything to pieces.

There is a lot of wind on the Alex, at the Tietz corner there is a lousy draft. A wind that blows between the houses and through the building excavations. It makes you feel you would like to hide in the saloons, but who can do that, it blows through your trousers pockets, then you notice something's happening, no monkey business, a man has got to be gay with this weather. Early in the morning the workers come tramping along from Reinickendorf, Neukölln, Weissensee. Cold or no cold, wind or no wind, we've gotta get the coffee pot, pack up the sandwiches, we've gotta work and slave, the drones sit on top, they sleep in their feather-beds and exploit us.

Aschinger has a big café and restaurant. People who have no belly, can get one there, people who have one already, can make it as big as they please. You cannot cheat Nature! Whoever thinks he can improve bread and pastry made from denatured white flour by the addition of artificial ingredients, deceives himself and the consumer. Nature has her laws of life and avenges every abuse. The decadent state of health of almost all civilized peoples today is caused by the use of denatured and artificially refined food. Fine sausages delivered to your house, liverwurst and blood-pudding cheap.

The highly interesting *Magazine*, instead of 1 mark, now only 20 pfennigs; *Marriage*, highly interesting and spicy, only 20 pfennigs. The newsboy puffs his cigarettes, he has a sailor's cap on, I beat everything.

From the east, Weissensee, Litchtenberg, Friedrichshain, Frankfurter Allee, the yellow street-cars plunge into the square through Landsberger Strasse. Line No. 65 comes from the Central Slaughter-House, the Gross Ring, Weddingplatz,

Luisenplatz; No. 76 from Hundekehle via Hubertusallee. At the corner of Landsberger Strasse they have sold out Friedrich Hahn, formerly a department store, they have emptied it and are gathering it to its forbears. The street-cars and Bus 19 stop on the Turmstrasse. Where Jürgens stationery store was, they have torn down the house and put up a building fence instead. An old man sits there with a medical scale: Try your weight, 5 pfennigs. Dear sisters and brethren, you who swarm across the Alex, give yourselves this treat, look through the loophole next to the medical scale at this dump-heap where Jürgens once flourished and where Hahn's department store still stands, emptied, evacuated, and eviscerated, with nothing but red tatters hanging over the show-windows. A dump-heap lies before us. Dust thou art, to dust returnest. We have built a splendid house, nobody comes in or goes out any longer. Thus Rome, Babylon, Nineveh, Hannibal, Caesar, all went to smash, oh, think of it! In the first place, I must remark they are digging those cities up again, as the illustrations in last Sunday's edition show, and, in the second place, those cities have fulfilled their purpose, and we can now build new cities. Do you cry about your old trousers when they are moldy and seedy? No, you simply buy new ones, thus lives the world.

The police tower over the square. Several specimens of them are standing about. Each specimen sends a connoisseur's glance to both sides, and knows the traffic rules by heart. It has putties around its legs, a rubber mace hangs from its right side, it swings its arms horizontally from west to east, and thus north and south, cannot advance any farther, east flows west, and west flows east. Then the specimen switches about automatically: north flows south, south flows north. The copper has a well-defined waist-line. As soon as he jerks around, there is a rush across the square in the direction of Königstrasse of about 30 private individuals, some of them stop on the traffic island, one part reaches the other side and continues walking on the planks. The same number have started east, they swim towards the others, the same thing has befallen them, but there was no mishap.

There are men, women, and children, the latter mostly holding women's hands. To enumerate them all and to describe their destinies is hardly possible, and only in a few cases would this succeed. The wind scatters chaff over all of them alike.

The faces of the eastward wanderers are in no way different from those of the wanderers to west, south, and north; moreover they exchange their rôles, those who are now crossing the square towards Aschinger's may be seen an hour later in front of the empty Hahn Department Store. Just as those who come from Brunnenstrasse on their way to Jannowitz Brücke mingle with those coming from the reverse direction. Yes, and many of them turn off to the side, from south to east, from south to west, from north to west, from north to east. They have the same equanimity as passengers in an omnibus or in street-cars. The latter all sit in different postures, making the weight of the car, as indicated outside, heavier still. Who could find out what is happening inside them, a tremendous chapter. And if anyone did write it, to whose advantage would it be? New books? Even the old ones don't sell, and in the year '27 book-sales as compared with '26 have declined so and so much per cent. Taken simply as private individuals, the people who paid 20 pfennigs, leaving out those possessing monthly tickets and pupils' cards—the latter only pay 10 pfennigs—are riding with their weight from a hundred to two hundred pounds, in their clothes, with pockets, parcels, keys, hats, sets of artificial teeth, trusses, riding across Alexanderplatz, holding those mysterious long tickets on which is written: Line 12 Siemensstrasse D A, Gotzkowskistrasse C, B, Oranienburger Tor C, C, Kottbuser Tor A, mysterious tokens, who can solve them, who can guess and who confess them, three words I tell you heavy with thought, and the scraps of paper are punched four times at certain places, and on them there is written in that same German in which the Bible and the Criminal Code are written: Valid till the end of the line, by the shortest route, connection with other lines not guaranteed. They read newspapers of various tendencies, conserve their balance by means of semicircular canals of their internal ear, inhale oxygen, stare stupidly at each other, have pains, or no pains, think, don't think, are happy, unhappy, are neither happy nor unhappy.

Rrrr, rrr, the pile-driver thumps down, I beat everything, another rail. Something is buzzing across the square coming from police headquarters, they are riveting, a cement crane dumps its load. Herr Adolf Kraun, house-servant, looks on, the tipping over of the wagon fairly fascinates him, you beat everything, he beats everything. He watches excitedly how the sand truck is always tilting up on one side, there it is up in the air, boom, and now it tips over. A fellow wouldn't like to be kicked out of bed like that, legs up, down with the head, there you lie, something might happen to him, but they do their job well, all the same.

Thomas Pynchon

GRAVITY'S RAINBOW

BACK TO BERLIN, with a terrific thunderstorm blowing
over the city. Margherita has brought Slothrop to a rickety
wood house near the Spree, in the Russian sector. A burned-
out Königstiger tank guards the entrance, its paint scorched,
treads mangled and blasted off of the drive sprocket, its
dead monster 88 angled down to point at the gray river,
hissing and spiculed with the rain.

Inside are bats nesting in the rafters, remains of

*Considered by many to be America's greatest living writer, Thomas Pynchon's liter-
ary reputation is equaled only by his desire for privacy. This passage from his 1973
masterpiece finds Tyrone Slothop in 1945 Berlin immediately following its demili-
tarization and division.*

beds with a moldy smell, broken glass and bat shit on the bare wood floor, windows boarded up except where the stove is vented through because the chimney's down. On a rocking chair lies a moleskin coat, a taupe cloud. Paint from some long-ago artist is still visible over the floor in wrinkled splashes of aged magenta, saffron, steel blue, reverse deformations of paintings whose whereabouts are unknown. Back in a corner hangs a tarnished mirror, birds and flowers painted in white all around its frame, reflecting Margherita and Slothrop and the rain out the open door. Part of the ceiling, blown away when the King Tiger died, is covered now with soggy and stained cardboard posters all of the same cloaked figure in the broad-brimmed hat, with its legend DER FEIND HÖRT ZU. Water drips through in half a dozen places.

Greta lights a kerosene lamp. It warms the rainlight with a handful of yellow. Slothrop builds a fire in the stove while Margherita ducks down under the house, where it turns out there's a great stash of potatoes. Jeepers, Slothrop hasn't seen a potato for months. There's onions in a sack too, and even wine. She cooks, and they both sit there just pigging on those spuds. Later, without paraphernalia or talk, they fuck each other to sleep. But a few hours later Slothrop wakes up, and lies there wondering where he's going.

Well, to find that Säure Bummer, soon as this rain lets up, give the man his hashish. But what then? Slothrop and the S-Gerät and the Jamf/Imipolex mystery have grown to be strangers. He hasn't really thought about them for a while. Hmm, when *was* that? The day he sat with Säure in the café, smoking that reefer . . . oh, that was day before yesterday, wasn't it? Rain drips, soaking into the floor, and Slothrop perceives that he is losing his mind. If there is something comforting—religious, if you want—about paranoia, there is still also anti-paranoia, where nothing is connected to anything, a condition not many of us can bear for long. Well right now Slothrop feels himself sliding onto the anti-paranoid part of his cycle, feels the whole city around him going back roofless, vulnerable, uncentered as he is, and only pasteboard images now of the Listening Enemy left between him and the wet sky.

Either They have put him here for a reason, or he's just here. He isn't sure that he wouldn't, actually, rather have that *reason*. . . .

The rain lets up at midnight. He leaves Margherita to creep out in the cold city with his five kilos, having kept for himself the one Tchitcherine plundered from. Russian troops are singing in their billets. The salt ache of accordion music cries on in back of them. Drunks materialize, merry and pissing in the center grooves of cobbled alleys. Mud occupies some streets like flesh. Shell craters brim with rainwater, gleaming in the lights of midwatch work crews clearing debris. Shattered Biedermeier chair, mateless boot, steel eyeglass frame, dog collar (eyes at the edges of the twisting trail watching her sign, for blazing), wine cork, splintered broom, bicycle with one wheel missing, discarded copies of *Tägliche Rundschau,* chalcedony doorknob dyed blue long ago with ferrous ferrocyanide, scattered piano keys (all white, an octave on B to be exact—or H, in the German nomenclature—the notes of the rejected Locrian mode), the black and amber eye from some stuffed animal. . . . The strewn night. Dogs, spooked and shivering, run behind walls whose tops are broken like fever charts. Somewhere a gas leak warps for a minute into the death and after-rain smells. Ranks of blackened window-sockets run high up the sides of gutted apartment buildings. Chunks of concrete are held aloft by iron reinforcing rods that curls like black spaghetti, whole enormous heaps wiggling ominously overhead at your least passing brush by. . . . The smooth-faced Custodian of the Night hovers behind neutral eyes and smile, coiled and pale over the city, humming its hoarse lullabies. Young men spent the Inflation like this, alone in the street, no place to go into out of the black winters. Girls stayed up late on stoops or sitting on benches in lamplight by the rivers, waiting for business, but the young men had to walk by, ignored, hunching overpadded shoulders, money with no relation to anything it could buy, swelling paper cancer in their billfolds. . . .

The Chicago Bar is being guarded outside by two of their descendants, kids in George Raft suits, many sizes too big, too many ever to grow into. One keeps coughing, in uncontrolled dying spasms. The other licks his lips and stares at Slothrop. Gunsels. When he mentions Säure Bummer's name, they move together in front of the door, shaking their heads. "Look, I'm supposed to deliver him a package."

"Don't know him."

"Can I leave a message?"

"He's not here." The cougher makes a lunge. Slothrop sweeps aside, gives him a quick veronica with his cape, sticks his foot out and trips the kid, who lies on the ground cursing, all tangled up in his long keychain, while his pardner goes pawing inside his flapping suitcoat for what Slothrop surmises to be a sidearm, so him Slothrop kicks in the balls, and screaming "Fickt nicht mit der Raketemensch!" so they'll remember, kind of hiyo Silver here, he flees into the shadows, among the heaps of lumber, stone and earth.

He takes a trail he thinks Säure led them along the other night—keeps losing it, wandering into windowless mazes, tangles of barbed wire holidayed by the death-storms of last May, then into a strafed and pitted lorry-park he can't find his way out of for half an hour, a rolling acre of rubber, grease, steel, and spilled petrol, pieces of vehicles pointing at sky or earth no differently than in a peacetime American junk-yard, fused into odd, brown *Saturday Evening Post* faces, except that they are not folksy so much as downright sinister . . . yes it's really the Saturday Evening *Post*, all right: they are the faces of the tricorned messengers coming in from out of the long pikes, down past the elms, Berkshire legends, travelers lost at the edge of the Evening. Come with a message. They unwrinkle, though, if you keep looking. They smooth out into timeless masks that speak their entire meaning, all of it right out on the surface.

It takes an hour to find Säure's cellar. But it's dark, and it's empty. Slothrop goes in, lights the light. Looks like either a bust or a gang war: printing press vanished, clothes tossed all around, and some very strange clothes at that, there is, for example, a wickerware suit, a *yellow* wickerware suit actually, articulating along armpit, elbow, knee and groinlines . . . oh, hmm, well, Slothrop runs a quick search of his own here, looking inside shoes, not really shoes, some of them, but footgloves with individual *toes*, not, however, sewn but *cast* from some unpleasant variegated resin such as bowling balls are made of . . . behind the peeling scraps of wallpaper, up in the rolled-up windowshade, among the hatchings of one or two phony Reichsmarks let spill by the looters—fifteen minutes of this, finding nothing . . . and the white object on the table watching him out of its staring shadows the whole time. He feels its stare before he spots it finally: a chesspiece two inches high. A white knight, molded out of plastic—a-and wait'll Slothrop finds out what *kind* of plastic, boy!

It's a horse's skull: the eye-sockets are hollow far down into the base. Inside one of them is a tightly rolled cigarette paper with a message from Säure. "Raketemensch! Der Springer asks me to give you this, his symbol. Keep it—by it shall he know you. I am at Jacobistrasse 12, 3er Hof, number 7. As B/4, Me. I?" Now "As B/4" was John Dillinger's old signoff. Everybody in the Zone this summer is using it. It indicates to people how you feel about certain things. . . .

Säure has included a map showing how to get to where he is. It's clear back in the British sector. Groaning, Slothrop pushes on back out in the mud and early morning. Around the Brandenburg Gate, a slight drizzle starts up again.

Chunks of the Gate still lie around in the street—leaning shell-spalled up in the rainy sky, its silence is colossal, haggard as he pads by flanking it, the Chariot gleaming like coal, driven and still, it is the 30th century and swashbuckling Rocketman has just landed here to tour the ruins, the high-desert traces of an ancient European order. . . .

The Jacobistrasse and most of its quarter, slums, survived the street-fighting intact, along with its interior darkness, a masonry of shadows that will persist whether the sun is up or down. Number 12 is an entire block of tenements dating from before the Inflation, five or six stories and a mansarde, five or six Hinterhöfe nested one inside the other—boxes of a practical joker's gift, nothing in the center but a last hollow courtyard smelling of the same cooking and garbage and piss decades old. Ha, ha!

Slothrop moseys toward the first archway. Streetlight throws his caped shadow forward into a succession of these arches, each labeled with a faded paint name, Erster-Hof, Zweiter-Hof, Dritter-Hof u.s.w., shaped like the entrance to the Mittelwerke, parabolic, but more like an open mouth and gullet, joints of cartilage receding waiting, waiting to swallow . . . above the mouth two squared eyes, organdy whites, irises pitch black, stare him down . . . it laughs as it has for years without stopping, a blubbery and percussive laugh, like heavy china rolling or bumping under the water in the sink. A brainless giggle, just big old geometric me, nothin' t' be nervous about, c'mon in. . . . But the pain, the twenty, twenty-five years of pain paralyzed back in that long throat . . . old outcast, passive, addicted to survival now, waiting the years out, waiting for vulnerable saps like Slothrop here to expose itself to, laughing and crying and all in silence . . . paint peels from the Face, burned, diseased, long time dying and how can Slothrop just walk down into such a schizoid throat? Why, because it is what the guardian and potent Studio wants from him, natürlich: Slothrop is the character juvenile tonight: what's kept him moving the whole night, him and the others, the solitary Berliners who come out only in these evacuated hours, belonging and going noplace, is Their unexplained need to keep some marginal population in these wan and preterite places, certainly for economic though, who knows, maybe emotional reasons too. . . .

Säure's on the move too, though inside, prowling his dreams. It looks like one big room, dark, full of tobacco and kif smoke, crumbled ridges of plaster where walls have been knocked out, straw pallets all over the floor, a couple on one sharing a late, quiet cigarette, somebody snoring on another . . . glossy Bosendorfer Imperial concert grand piano over which Trudi, wearing only an army shirt, leans, a desperate muse, bare legs long and stretching, *"Please* come to bed Gustav, it'll be light soon." The only answer is a peevish strumming among the lower strings. Säure is on his side, quite still, a shrunken child, face long worked at by leaps from second-story windows, "first rubdowns" under gloved and womanish sergeants' fists in the precinct stations, golden light in the afternoons over the racetrack at Karlshorst, black light from the pavements of boulevards at night finely wrinkled like leather stretched over stone, white light from satin dresses, glasses stacked shining in front of bar mirrors, sans-serif Us at the entrances to underground stations pointing in smooth magnetism at the sky to bring down steel angels of exaltation, of languid surrender—a face that in sleep is awesomely old, abandoned to its city's history. . . .

His eyes open—for an instant Slothrop is only shadowed green folds, highlighted helmet, light-values still to be put together. Then comes the sweet nodding smile, everything's O.K., ja, howdy Rocketman, was ist los? Though the unregenerate old doper is not quite kindly enough to keep from opening the ditty bag right away and peering in, eyes like two pissholes in a snowbank, to see what he has.

"I thought you'd be in the slam or something."

Out with a little Moroccan pipe and Säure sets to flattening a fat crumb of that hashish, humming the popular rumba

A little something from Moroc-co,
With just a lit-tle bit of sock-o,

"Oh. Well, Springer blew the whistle on our counterfeiting operation. Kind of a little temporary hitch, you understand."

"I don't. You're supposed to be ace buddies."

"Not nearly. And he moves in higher orbits." It is something very complicated having to do with American yellow-seal scrip being discontinued in the Mediterranean theatre, with the reluctance of Allied forces here to accept Reichsmarks. Springer has a balance-of-payments problem too, and he's been speculating heavily in Sterling, and . . .

"But," sez Slothrop, "but, uh, where's my million marks, then, Emil?"

Säure sucks yellow flame flowing over the edge of the bowl. "It is gone where the woodbine twineth." Exactly what Jubilee Jim Fisk told the Congressional committee investigating his and Jay Gould's scheme to corner gold in 1869. The words are a reminder of Berkshire. With nothing more than that to go on, it occurs to Slothrop that Säure can't possibly be on the Bad Guys' side. Whoever They are, Their game has been to extinguish, not remind.

"Well, I can sell by the ounce from what I have," Slothrop reckons. "For occupation scrip. That's stable, isn't it?"

"You aren't angry. You really aren't."

"Rocketman is above all that shit, Emil."

"I have a surprise for you. I can get you the Schwarzgerät you asked about."

"You?"

"Springer. I asked him for you."

"Quit fooling. Really? Jeepers, that's so swell of you! How can I—"

"Ten thousand pounds sterling."

Slothrop loses a whole lungful of smoke. "Thanks Emil. . . ." He tells Säure about the run-in with Tchitcherine, and also about how he saw that Mickey Rooney.

"Rocketman! Spaceman! Welcome to our virgin planet. We only want to be left in some kind of peace here, O.K.? If you kill us, don't eat us. If you eat, don't digest. Let us come out the other end again, like diamonds in the shit of smugglers. . . ."

"Look"—remembering now the tip that Geli gave him long ago in Nordhausen—"did your pal Springer mention he was hanging out in Swinemünde these days, anyplace like that?"

"Only the price of your instrument, Rak. Half the

money in front. He said it would cost him at least that much to track it down."

"So he doesn't know where it is. Shit, he could have us all on the hook, bidding us up, hoping somebody's fool enough to front him some dough."

"Usually he delivers. You didn't have any trouble, did you, with that pass he forged?"

"Yaaahhh—" Oh. Oh, wow, aha, yes been meaning to ask you about this little Max Schlepzig item here—"Now then." But meantime Trudi has abandoned Gustav in the piano and comes over to sit and rub her cheeks against the nap of Slothrop's trousers, dear naked legs whispering together, hair spilling, shirt half unbuttoned, and Säure has at some point rolled over and gone groaning back into sleep. Trudi and Slothrop retire to a mattress well away from the Bosendorfer. Slothrop settles back sighing, takes his helmet off and lets big sweet and saftig Trudi have her way with him. His joints are aching with rain and city wandering, he's half blitzed, Trudi kissing him into an amazing comfort, it's an open house here, no favored senses or organs, all are equally at play . . .

for possibly the first time in his life Slothrop does not feel obliged to have a hardon, which is just as well, because it does not seem to be happening with his penis as much as with . . . oh mercy, this is embarrassing but . . . well his *nose* actually seems to be erecting, the mucus beginning to flow yes a nasal hardon here and Trudi has certainly noticed all right, how could she help but . . . as she slides her lips over the throbbing snoot and sends a yard of torrid tongue up one of his nostrils . . . he can feel each pink taste-bud as she penetrates even farther, pulling inside the vestibule walls and nose-hair now to accommodate her head, then shoulders and . . . well she's halfway in, might as well—pulling up her knees, crawling using the hair for hand and footholds she is able to stand at last inside the great red hall which is quite pleasantly lit, no walls or ceiling she can really discern but rather a fading to seashell and springtime grades of pink in all directions. . . .

They fall asleep in the roomful of snoring, with low-pitched twangs out of the piano, and the rain's million-legged scuttle in the courtyards outside. When Slothrop wakes up it's at the height of the Evil Hour, Trudi is in some other room with Gustav rattling coffee cups, a tortoise-shell cat chases flies by the dirty window. Back beside the Spree, the White Woman is waiting for Slothrop. He isn't especially disposed to leave. Trudi and Gustav come in with coffee and half a reefer, and everybody sits around gabbing.

Gustav is a composer. For months he has been carrying on a raging debate with Säure over who is better, Beethoven or Rossini. Säure is for Rossini. "I'm not so much for Beethoven qua Beethoven," Gustav argues, "but as he represents the German dialectic, the incorporation of more and more notes into the scale, culminating with dodecaphonic democracy, where all notes get an equal hearing. Beethoven was one of the architects of musical freedom—he submitted to the demands of history, despite his deafness. While Rossini was retiring at the age of 36, womanizing and getting fat, Beethoven was living a life filled with tragedy and grandeur."

"So?" is Säure's customary answer to that one. "Which would you rather do? The point is," cutting off Gustav's usually indignant scream, "a person feels *good* listening to Rossini. All you feel like listening to Beethoven is going out and invading Poland. Ode to Joy indeed. The man didn't even have a sense of humor. I tell you," shaking his skinny old fist, "there is more of the Sublime in the snare drum part to *La Gazza Ladra* than in the whole Ninth Symphony. With Rossini, the whole point is that lovers always get together, isolation is overcome, and like it or not that is the one great centripetal movement of the World. Through the machineries of greed, pettiness, and the abuse of power, *love occurs.* All the shit is transmuted to gold. The walls are breached, the balconies are scaled—listen!" It was a night in early May, and the final bombardment of Berlin was in progress. Säure had to shout his head off. "The Italian girl is in Algiers, the Barber's in the crockery, the magpie's stealing everything in sight! The World is rushing together. . . ."

This rainy morning, in the quiet, it seems that Gustav's German Dialectic has come to its end. He has just had the word, all the way from Vienna along some musicians' grapevine, that Anton Webern is dead. "Shot in May, by the Americans. Senseless, accidental if you believe in accidents— some mess cook from North Carolina, some late draftee with a .45 he hardly knew how to use, too late for WW II, but not for Webern. The excuse for raiding the house was that Webern's brother was in the black market. Who isn't? Do you know what kind of myth *that's* going to make in a thousand years? The young barbarians coming in to murder the Last European, standing at the far end of what'd been going on since Bach, an expansion of music's polymorphous perversity till all notes were truly equal at last. . . . Where was there to go after Webern? It was the moment of maximum freedom. It all had to come down. Another Götterdämmerung—"

"Young fool," Säure now comes cackling in from out in Berlin, trailing a pillowcase full of flowering tops just in from that North Africa. He's a mess—red-drenched eyes, fatbaby arms completely hairless, fly open and half the buttons gone, white hair and blue shirt both streaked with some green horrible scum. "Fell in a shell-hole. Here, quick, roll up some of this."

"What do you mean, 'young fool,' " inquires Gustav.

"I mean you and your musical mainstreams," cries Säure. "Is it finally over? Or do we have to start da capo with Carl Orff?"

"I never thought of that," sez Gustav, and for a moment it is clear that Säure has heard about Webern too, and trying in his underhanded way to cheer Gustav up.

"What's wrong with *Rossini?*" hollers Säure, lighting up. "*Eh?*"

"Ugh," screams Gustav, "ugh, ugh, Rossini," and they're at it again, "you wretched antique. Why doesn't anybody go to concerts any more? You think it's because of the war? *Oh no, I'll* tell you why, old man—because the halls are full of people like you! *Stuffed* full! Half asleep, nodding and smiling, farting through their dentures, hawking and spitting into paper bags, dreaming up ever more ingenious plots against their children—not just their own, but *other people's* children too! just sitting around, at the concert with all these other snow-topped old rascals, just a nice background murmur of wheezing, belching, intestinal gurgles, scratching, sucking, croaking, and entire opera house crammed full of them right up to standing room, they're doddering in the aisles, hanging off the tops of the highest balconies, and you know what they're *all listening to,* Säure?

eh? They're all listening to Rossini! Sitting there drooling away to some medley of predictable little tunes, leaning forward elbows on knees muttering, 'C'mon, c'mon then Rossini, let's get all this pretentious fanfare stuff out of the way, let's get on to the *real good tunes!*' Behavior as shameless as eating a whole jar of peanut butter at one sitting. On comes the sprightly *Tancredi* tarantella, and they stamp their feet in delight, they pop their teeth and pound their canes—'Ah, ah! *that's* more like it!' "

"It's a *great* tune," yells Säure back. "Smoke another one of these and I'll just play it for you here on the Bosendorfer."

To the accompaniment of this tarantella, which really is a good tune, Magda has come in out of the morning rain, and is now rolling reefers for everybody. She hands Säure one to light. He stops playing and peers at it for a long time. Nodding now and then, smiling or frowning.

Gustav tends to sneer, but Säure really turns out to be an adept at the difficult art of papyromancy, the ability to prophesy through contemplating the way people roll reefers—the shape, the licking pattern, the wrinkles and folds or absence thereof in the paper. "You will soon be in love," sez Säure, "see, this line here."

"It's long, isn't it? Does that mean——"

"Length is usually intensity. Not time."

"Short but sweet," Magda sighs. "Fabelhaft, was?" Trudi comes over to hug her. They are a Mutt and Jeff routine, Trudi in heels is a foot or so taller. They know how it looks, and travel around the city together whenever they can, by way of intervening, if only for a minute, in people's minds.

"How do you like this shit?" sez Säure.

"*Hübsch,*" allows Gustav. "A trifle *stahlig,* and perhaps the infinitesimal hint of a *Bodengeschmack* behind its *Körper,* which is admittedly *süffig.*"

"I would rather have said *spritzig,*" Säure disagrees, if that indeed is what it is. "Generally more *bukettreich* than last year's harvests, wouldn't you say?"

"Oh, for an Haut Atlas herbage it does have its *Art.* Certainly it can be described as *kernig,* even—as can often be said of that *sauber* quality prevailing in the Oued Nfis region—authentically *pikant.*"

"Actually I would tend to suspect an origin somewhere along the southern slope of Jebel Sarho," Säure sez—"note the *Spiel*, rather *glatt* and *blumig*, even the suggestion of a *Fülle* in its *würzig* audacity—"

"No no no, *Fülle* is overstating it, the El Abid Emerald we had last month had *Fülle*. But this is obviously more *zart* than that."

The truth is they are both so blitzed that neither one knows what he's talking about, which is just as well, for at this point comes a godawful hammering at the door and a lot of achtungs from the other side. Slothrop screams and heads for the window, out onto the roof and over, scrambling down a galvanized pipe to the next streetward courtyard. Back in Säure's room the heat come busting in. Berlin police supported by American MPs in an advisor status.

"You will show me your papers!" hollers the leader of the raid.

Säure smiles and holds up a pack of Zig-Zags, just in from Paris.

Franz Kafka

PICTURE POSTCARD, BERLIN

DEAREST MAX,

The difference is this: in Paris one is cheated, here one cheats; it is sort of comical. On Saturday I went almost directly from the train to the Kammerspiele; I've acquired a taste for buying tickets in advance. Today I am going to see *Anatol.*[1] But nothing is as good as food in the vegetarian restaurant here. The place itself is a little dreary; people eating fried eggs and cabbage (the most expensive dish); the

---

The prolific, enigmatic novelist Franz Kafka requested that his entire writings be destroyed upon his death. Fortunately, his friend Max Brod disobeyed his instructions. This postcard is from his surprisingly content holiday in Berlin, as reprinted in Letters to Friends, Family, and Editors.

architecture is nothing; but what contentment one feels here. I keep sounding my inner state; at the moment, to be sure, I still feel very bad, but how will I feel tomorrow? This place is so thoroughly vegetarian that even tips are forbidden. Instead of rolls, there is only Simons' bread.[2] Right now the waiter is bringing me semolina pudding with raspberry syrup. But I am also having lettuce with cream, which will go well with gooseberry wine, and I'll finish off with a cup of strawberry-leaf tea.

[1] Arthur Schnitzler's (1862–1931) first play (1893).
[2] A special whole-grain bread baked for twelve hours at low heat, introduced by Simons of Soest, Westphalia. It is still on the market.

Marcellus Schiffer

THE LAVENDER LAY

How civilized
That we're despised
And treated as something taboo,
Though wise and good, 'cause our selfhood
Is special through and through.
We're classified
Fit to be tried,
For the law forbids us too.

In Weimar Berlin, gay and lesbian cabarets were famous enough to be included on the route of Cook's tours. Marcellus Schiffer (1892-1932) was one of the more popular cabaret writers; this song is one of his best.

Since we're of different stripe,
They malign and fine our type.

REFRAIN:
After all, we're different from the others
Who only love in lockstep with morality,
Who wander blinkered through a world of wonders,
And find their fun in nothing but banality.
We don't know what it is to feel that way,
In our own world we're sisters and we're brothers:
We love the night, so lavender, so gay,
For, after all, we're different from the others!

Why the quarrels
Others' morals
Foist on us, torment bringing?
We, near and far,
Are what we are.
They'd love to see us swinging.
But still we think

Were we to swing,

You'd soon hear them complain,

For, sad their plight,

In just one night,

Our sun would shine again.

For equal rights we fought our bitter war!

We *will* be tolerated, and never suffer more!!

REFRAIN (*repeat*)

Bennett Owen

THE PARTY AT THE WALL

WEST BERLIN—IT began as a trickle. On East German TV, a government spokesman had ended an evening press conference by saying that citizens of the GDR could travel freely, and by 9:30 P.M. on November 9, the first East Berliners strolled across a bridge at Bornholmer Strasse. They'd heard the news in a bar and walked down to the nearest crossing to see if it was really true. It was. A small crowd greeted them as they reached the Western side. "May I come in?" asked one politely.

Bennett Owen's 1989 National Review *piece captures the energy and excitement that followed the momentous events of November 9, 1989. Owen is an editor at RIAS-TV in Berlin.*

"To walk across this bridge into West Berlin is the most normal thing in the world," one man said—and then added, "things haven't been normal here for 28 years." A youngster coming across pointed to the Wall he'd just passed through and commented, "This used to be the end of the world for us." At first, most said they just wanted to come over and walk on the Kurfürstendamm, Berlin's answer to Fifth Avenue. But as the news spread, the border crossings quickly became jammed with people. The soldiers who once had orders to shoot to kill were reduced to stamping passports and directing traffic. They laughed when they asked if they'd been handed their pink slips yet. By midnight, the celebration had begun in earnest. Thousands of Germans from East and West gathered at the Brandenburg Gate, drinking cheap champagne just steps away from crosses commemorating those whose dreams of freedom couldn't wait this long.

"I have seen the future and it runs through the heart of Berlin." Through that kind of graffiti the Berlin Wall spoke with cynical eloquence, and last January, in the icy half-light of winter in Berlin, it appeared to say that the cold war was as cold as ever. George Shultz, on a final tour of Europe as Secretary of State, declared the Wall should come down. East Germany's Erich Honecker defiantly replied that it would be standing one hundred years from now, and at the same time a series of incidents dramatically underscored his words. Two young men who tried to flee across the Wall in the southern part of town were shot (one of them fatally), and in the days following, more shots were heard at border crossings in other parts of the city. In late January a man tried to swim to the West across the River Spree in the center of town. He made it to the western shore but was exhausted, and as he tried to pull himself from the water East German soldiers pulled him into their patrol boat by the hair. The border guards were taking their orders from the East German chief of security, a dedicated Marxist by the name of Egon Krenz.

Despite the show of force, escape attempts were a daily occurrence. Of the dozens who tried through the winter and spring of this year, two spectacular attempts come to mind. In one, a would-be escapee was killed when he fell from a makeshift hot-air balloon. In another, two brothers living in

West Germany flew two ultralight planes into East Germany where they picked up a third brother and flew him back to freedom. By the end of summer, though, that kind of desperation had evaporated as East Germans by the hundreds of thousands made an end-run through Hungary and Czechoslovakia. Egon Krenz became the new leader of East Germany, but, as a West German magazine put it, he is a shepherd without a flock. Desperately (and futilely, as later events have shown) seeking to regain control of his people, he threw open the Berlin Wall.

And so, on a crisp autumn night, a newspaper headline screams, "Berlin is Berlin again." Just after midnight on November 10, a very stout and very drunk reveler climbed onto the wall and, with the Brandenburg Gate as a backdrop, withstood the East German water cannon that tried to force him off. In freezing weather, he turned his back to the jets of water, and when the guards finally gave up, he turned toward them, unzipped his fly and . . . well, you know. As dramatic symbolism it doesn't quite equal staring down a tank in Tianammon Square, but the Germans applauded wildly.

By Friday evening, Berlin was pure and simple chaos, its population swollen by a half-million East Germans with more pouring in every minute. At Checkpoint Charlie, a seemingly unending river of champagne poured over the cars as they came through, and the mood was euphoric. On the dark and muddy pathway that follows the wall from Checkpoint Charlie to the Brandenburg Gate, there was a constant clinking of claw-hammers against cement as Berliners chipped away souvenirs. In the morning, jackhammers would take their place, opening up new crossings and making old roads and rail lines whole again. The surest sign that history was being made was at the Brandenburg Gate, where, thirty feet above the throngs of people in a cherry-picker, stood Dan Rather speaking into a video camera. Back on earth were ABC and NBC, and CNN seemed to be everywhere at once. By Saturday, more than a million guests had invaded Berlin—a newspaper cartoon showed an East German family running through a checkpoint, with a caption that read, "Quick, before the West Germans build a wall."

The most emotional event took place Sunday, when the Wall fell at Potsdamer Platz. The rest of the world sees the

Brandenburg Gate as the symbol of Berlin, but those who live here remember Potsdamer Platz as the heart of the old city. It was there where, in 1945, Soviet tanks crushed the last life out of the Third Reich, and where, in 1953, the uprising of June 17 was quelled. Now, the army that built the Wall is busy tearing holes in it. As Mayor Walter Momper declared, "The heart of Berlin will soon beat again."

Lillian Hellman

JULIA

I HAVE HERE changed most of the names. I don't know that it matters anymore, but I believe the heavy girl on the train still lives in Cologne and I am not sure that even now the Germans like their premature anti-Nazis. More important, Julia's mother is still living and so, perhaps, is Julia's daughter. Almost certainly, the daughter's father lives in San Francisco.

American dramatist Lillian Hellman spent much of her later years refining her memoirs, including this piece from her collection Pentimento: A Book of Portraits. *She lived out her days in New England, collaborating occasionally with her longtime companion, Dashiell Hammett.*

IN 1937, AFTER I had written *The Children's Hour* and *Days to Come,* I had an invitation to attend a theatre festival in Moscow. Whenever in the past I wrote about that journey, I omitted the story of my trip through Berlin because I did not feel able to write about Julia.

Dorothy Parker and her husband, Alan Campbell, were going to Europe that same August, and so we crossed together on the old *Normandie,* a pleasant trip even though Campbell, and his pretend-good-natured feminine jibes, had always made me uneasy.

When we reached Paris I was still undecided about going on to Moscow. I stayed around, happy to meet Gerald and Sara Murphy for the first time, Hemingway, who came up from Spain, and James Lardner, Ring Lardner's son, who was soon to enlist in the International Brigade and lost his life in Spain a few months later.

I liked the Murphys. I was always to like and be interested in them, but they were not for me what they had been to an older generation. They were, possibly, all that Calvin Tomkins says in his biography: they had style, Gerald had wit,

Sara grace and shrewdness, and that summer, soon after they had lost both their sons, they had a sweet dignity. But through the many years I was to see them after that I came to believe they were not as bonny as others thought them, or without troubles with each other, and long before the end—the end of my knowing them, I mean, a few years before Gerald died, when they saw very few of their old friends—I came to think that too much of their lives had been based on style. Style is mighty pleasant for those who benefit from it, but maybe not always rewarding for those who make and live by its necessarily strict rules.

There were many other people that summer in Paris, famous and rich, who invited Dottie for dinners and country lunches and tennis she didn't play and pools she didn't swim in. It gave me pleasure then, and forever after, that people courted her. I was amused at her excessive good manners, a kind of put-on, often there to hide contempt and dislike for those who flattered her at the very minute she begged for the flattery. When she had enough to drink the good manners got so good they got silly, but then the words came funny and sharp to show herself, and me, I think, that nobody could buy her. She was wrong: they could and did buy her for years. But they only bought a limited ticket to her life and in the end she died on her own road.

It was a new world for me. I had been courted around New York and Hollywood, as is everybody who has been a success in the theatre and young enough not to have been too much on display. But my invitations were second-class stuff compared to Dottie's admirers that month in Paris. I had a fine time, one of the best of my life. But one day, after a heavy night's drinking, I didn't anymore. I was a child of the Depression, a kind of Puritan Socialist, I guess—although to give it a name is to give it a sharper outline than it had—and I was full of the strong feelings the early Roosevelt period brought to many people. Dottie had the same strong feelings about something we all thought of as society and the future, but the difference between us was more than generational—she was long accustomed to much I didn't want. It was true that she always turned against the famous and rich who attracted her, but I never liked them well enough to bother that much.

I had several times that month spoken on the phone with my beloved childhood friend Julia, who was studying medicine in Vienna, and so the morning after the heavy drinking I called Julia to say I would come to Vienna the next day en route to Moscow. But that same night, very late, she called back.

She said, "I have something important for you to do. Maybe you'll do it, maybe you can't. But please stay in Paris for a few days and a friend will come to see you. If things work as I hope, you'll decide to go straight to Moscow by way of Berlin and I'll meet you on your way back."

When I said I didn't understand, who was the friend, why Berlin, she said, "I can't answer questions. Get a German visa tomorrow. You'll make your own choice, but don't talk about it now."

It would not have occurred to me to ignore what Julia told me to do because that's the way it had always been between us. So I went around the next morning to the German consulate for a visa. The consul said they'd give me a traveling permit, but would not allow me to stay in Berlin overnight, and the Russia consul said that wasn't unusual for people en route to Moscow.

I waited for two days and was about to call Julia again on the day of the morning I went down for an early breakfast in the dining room of the Hotel Meurice. (I had been avoiding Dottie and Alan, all invitations, and was troubled and annoyed by two snippy, suspicious notes from Alan about what was I up to, why was I locked in my room?) The concierge said the gentleman on the bench was waiting for me. A tall middle-aged man got up from the bench and said, "Madame Hellman? I come to deliver your tickets and to talk with you about your plans. Miss Julia asked me to call with the travel folders."

We went into the dining room, and when I asked him what he would like he said, in German, "Do you think I can have an egg, hot milk, a roll? I cannot pay for them."

When the waiter moved away, the tall man said, "You must not understand German again. I made a mistake."

I said I didn't understand enough German to worry anybody, but he didn't answer me and took to reading the travel folders until the food came. Then he ate very fast, smiling as he did it, as if he were remembering something pleasant from long ago past. When he finished, he handed me a note. The note said, "This is my friend, Johann. He will tell you. But *I* tell you, don't push yourself. If you can't you can't, no dishonor. Whatever, I will meet you soon. Love, Julia."

Mr. Johann said, "I thank you for fine breakfast. Could we walk now in Tuileries?"

As we entered the gardens he asked me how much I knew about Benjamin Franklin, was I an expert? I said I knew almost nothing. He said he admired Franklin and perhaps someday I could find him a nice photograph of Franklin in America. He sat down suddenly on a bench and mopped his forehead on this cool, damp day.

"Have you procured a German visa?"

"A traveling visa. I cannot stay overnight. I can only change stations in Berlin for Moscow."

"Would you carry for us fifty thousand dollars? We think, we do not guarantee, you will be without trouble. You will be taking the money to enable us to bribe out many already in prison, many who soon will be. We are a small group, valuable workers against Hitler. We are of no common belief or religion. The people who will meet you for the money, if your consent is given, were once small publishers. We are of Catholic, Communist, many beliefs. Julia has said that I must remind you for her that you are afraid of being afraid, and so will do what sometimes you cannot do, and that could be dangerous to you and to us."

I took to fiddling with things in my pocketbook, lit a cigarette, fiddled some more. He sat back as if he were very tired, and stretched.

After a while I said, "Let's go and have a drink."

He said, "I repeat. We think all will go well, but much could go wrong. Julia says I must tell you that, but that if we should not hear from you by the time of Warsaw, Julia will use her family with the American ambassador there through Uncle John."

"I know her family. There was a time she didn't believe in them much."

"She said you would note that. And so to tell you that her Uncle John is now governor. He does not like her but did not refuse her money for his career. And that her mother's last divorce has made her mother dependent on Julia as well."

I laughed at this picture of Julia controlling members of her very rich family. I don't think we had seen each other more than ten or twelve times since we were eighteen years old and so the years had evidently brought changes I didn't know about. Julia had left college, gone to Oxford, moved on to medical school in Vienna, had become a patient-pupil of Freud's. We had once, in the last ten years, spent a Christmas holiday together, and one summer, off Massachusetts, we had sailed for a month on her small boat, but in the many letters we had written in those years neither of us knew much more than the bare terms of each other's life, nothing of the daily stuff that is the real truth, the importance.

I knew, for example, that she had become, maybe always was, a Socialist, and lived by it, in a one-room apartment in a slum district of Vienna, sharing her great fortune with whoever needed it. She allowed herself very little, wanted very little. Oddly, gifts to me did not come into the denial: they were many and extravagant. Through the years, whenever she saw anything I might like, it was sent to me: old Wedgwood pieces, a Toulouse-Lautrec drawing, a fur-lined coat we saw together in Paris, a set of Balzac that she put in a rare Empire desk, and a wonderful set of Georgian jewelry, I think the last thing she could have had time to buy.

I said to the gray man, "Could I think it over for a few hours? That's what Julia meant."

He said, "Do not think hard. It is best not to be too prepared for matters of this kind. I will be at the station tomorrow morning. If you agree to carry the money, you will say hello to me. If you have decided it is not right for you, pass by me. Do not worry whichever is decided by you." He held out his hand, bowed, and moved away from me across the gardens.

I spent the day in and around Sainte-Chapelle, tried to eat lunch and dinner, couldn't, and went back to the hotel to pack only after I was sure Dottie and Alan would have gone to dinner with the Murphys. I left a note for them saying I was leaving early in the morning and would find them again after Moscow. I knew I had spent the whole day in a mess of indecision. Now I lay down, determined that I would not sleep until I had taken stock of myself. But decisions, particularly important ones, have always made me sleepy, perhaps because I know that I will have to make them by instinct, and thinking things out is only what other people tell me I should do. In any case, I slept through the night and rose only in time to hurry for the early morning train.

I was not pleased to find Dottie and Alan in the lobby, waiting to take me to the station. My protests were so firm and so awkward that Alan, who had a remarkable nose for deception, asked if I had a reason for not wanting them to come with me. When he went to get a taxi, I said to Dottie, "Sorry if I sounded rude. Alan makes me nervous."

She smiled, "Dear Lilly, you'd be a psychotic if he didn't."

At the railroad station I urged them to leave me when my baggage was carried on, but something had excited Alan: perhaps my nervousness; certainly not his claim that they had never before known anybody who was en route to Moscow. He was full of bad jokes about what I must not say to Russian actors, how to smuggle out caviar, and all the junk people like Alan say when they want to say something else.

I saw the gray man come down the platform. As he came near us Alan said, "Isn't that the man I saw you with in the Tuileries yesterday?" And as I turned to say something to Alan, God knows what it would have been, the gray man went past me and was moving back into the station.

I ran toward him. "Mr. Johann. Please, Mr. Johann." As he turned, I lost my head and screamed, "Please don't go away. *Please.*"

He stood still for what seemed like a long time, frowning. Then he moved slowly back toward me, as if he were coming with caution, hesitation.

Then I remembered: I said, "I only wanted to say hello. Hello to you, Mr. Johann, hello."

"Hello, Madam Hellman."

Alan had come to stand near us. Some warning had to be made. "This is Mr. Campbell and Miss Parker there. Mr. Campbell says he saw us yesterday and now he will ask me who you are and say that he didn't know we knew each other so well that you would come all this way to say goodbye to me."

Mr. Johann said, without hesitation, "I wish I could say that was true. But I have come to search for my nephew who is en route to Poland. He is not in his coach, he is late, as is his habit. His name is W. Franz, car 4, second class, and if I do not find him I would be most grateful if you say to him I came." He lifted his hat. "I am most glad, Madame Hellman, that we had this chance to say hello."

"Oh, yes," I said, "indeed. Hello. Hello."

When he was gone, Alan said, "What funny talk. You're talking like a foreigner."

"Sorry," I said, "sorry not to speak as well as you do in Virginia."

Dottie laughed, I kissed her and jumped for the train. I was nervous and went in the wrong direction. By the time a conductor told me where my compartment was, the train had left the station. On the connecting platform, before I reached my coach, a young man was standing holding a valise and packages. He said, "I am W. Franz, nephew, car 4, second class. This is a birthday present from Miss Julia." He handed me a box of candy and a hatbox marked "Madame Pauline." Then he bowed and moved off.

I carried the boxes to my compartment, where two young women were sitting on the left bench. One girl was small and thin and carried a cane. The other was a big-boned woman of about twenty-eight, in a heavy coat, wrapped tight against this mild day. I smiled at them, they nodded, and I sat down. I put the packages next to me and only then noticed that there was a note pasted on the hat-box. I was frightened of it, thought about taking it to the ladies' room, decided that would look suspicious, and opened it. I had a good memory in those days for poems, for what people said, for the looks of things, but it has long since been blurred by time. But I still remember every word of that note: "At the border, leave the candy box on the seat.

Open this box and wear the hat. There is no thanks for what you will do for them. No thanks from me either. But there is the love I have for you. Julia."

I sat for a long time holding the note. I was in a state that I have known since I was old enough to know myself, and that to this day frightens me and makes me unable even to move my hands. I do not mean to be foolishly modest about my intelligence: it is often high, but I have known since childhood that faced with a certain kind of simple problem, I sometimes make it so complex that there is no way out. I simply do not see what another mind grasps immediately. I was there now. Julia had not told me where to open the hatbox. To take it into the corridor or toilet might make the two ladies opposite me suspicious. And so I sat doing nothing for a long time until I realized that I didn't know when we crossed the border—a few minutes or a few hours. A decision had to be made but I could not make it.

BUT ON THAT day in 1937, on the train moving toward the German border, I sat looking at the hatbox. The big girl was now reading the *Frankfurter Zeitung,* the thin girl had done nothing with the book that was lying on her lap. I suppose it was the announcement of the first lunch sitting that made me look up from the past, pick up my coat, and then put it down again.

The thin girl said, "Nice coat. Warm? Of what fur?"

"It's sealskin. Yes, it's warm."

She said, pointing to the hatbox, "Your hat is also fur?"

I started to say I didn't know, realized how paralyzed I had been, knew it couldn't continue, and opened the box. I took out a high, fluffy, hat of gray fox as both ladies murmured their admiration. I sat staring at it until the heavy girl said, "Put on. Nice with coat."

I suppose part of my worry, although I hadn't even got there yet, was what to do with the knitted cap I was wearing. I took it off and rose to fix the fur hat in the long mirror between the windows. The top and sides of the hat were heavy and when I put my hands inside I felt a deep seam in the lining with heavy wads below and around the seam. It was uncomfortable and so I started to take it off when I remembered that the note said I should wear the hat.

Somewhere during my hesitations the heavy girl said she was going to lunch, could she bring me a sandwich? I said I'd rather go to lunch but I didn't know when we crossed the border, and immediately realized I had made a silly and possibly dangerous remark. The thin girl said we wouldn't be crossing until late afternoon—she had unpacked a small box and was eating a piece of meat—and if I was worried about my baggage she would stay in the compartment because she couldn't afford the prices in the dining car. The heavy girl said she couldn't afford them either, but the doctor had said she must have hot meals and a glass of wine with her medicine. So I went off with her to the dining car, leaving my coat thrown over the candy box. We sat at a table with two other people and she told me that she had been studying in Paris, had "contracted" a lung ailment, and was going home to Cologne. She said she didn't know what would happen to her Ph.D. dissertation because the lung ailment had affected her bones. She talked in a disjointed stream of words for the benefit, I thought, of the two men who sat next to us, but even when they left, the chatter went on as her head turned to watch everybody in a nervous tic between sentences. I was glad to be finished with lunch, so worried was I about the candy box, but it was there, untouched, when we got back to our compartment. The thin girl was asleep, but she woke up as we came in and said something in German to the heavy girl about a crowded train, and called her Louisa. It was the first indication I had that they knew each other, and I sat silent for a long time wondering why that made me uneasy. Then I told myself that if everything went on making be nervous, I'd be in a bad fix by the time it came to be nervous.

For the next few hours, the three of us dozed or read until the thin girl tapped me on the knee and said we would be crossing the border in five or ten minutes. I suppose everybody comes to fear in a different way, but I have always grown very hot or very cold, and neither has anything to do with the weather. Now, waiting, I was very hot. As the train pulled to a standstill, I got up to go outside—people were already leaving the train to pass through a check gate, and men were coming on the train to inspect baggage in the cars ahead of us—without my coat or my new hat. I was almost out the compartment door when the thin girl said, "You will need your coat and hat. It is of a windiness."

"Thank you. But I'm not cold."

Her voice changed sharply, "You will have need of your coat. Your hat is nice on your head."

I didn't ask questions because the tone in which she spoke was the answer. I turned back, put the coat around my shoulders, put on the hat that felt even heavier now with the wads of something that filled the lining, and let both girls go past me as I adjusted it in the mirror. Coming out on the platform, they were ahead of me, separated from me by several people who had come from other compartments. The heavy girl moved on. The thin girl dropped her purse and, as she picked it up, stepped to one side and moved directly behind me. We said nothing as we waited in line to reach the two uniformed men at the check gate. As the man in front of me was having his passport examined, the thin girl said, "If you have a temporary travel-through visa, it might take many minutes more than others. But that is nothing. Do not worry."

It didn't take many minutes more than others. I went through as fast as anybody else, turned in a neat line with the other travelers and went back to the train. The thin girl was directly behind me, but as we got to the steps of the train, she said, "Please," and pushed me aside to climb in first. When we reached our compartment, the fat girl was in her seat listening to two customs men in the compartment next to ours as they had some kind of good-natured discussion with a man who was opening his luggage.

The thin girl said, "They are taking great time with the luggage." As she spoke, she leaned over and picked up my candy box. She took off the ribbon and said, "Thank you. I am hungry for a chocolate. Most kind."

I said, "Please, please," and I knew I was never meant for this kind of thing. "I am carrying it to a friend for a gift. Please do not open it." As the customs men came into our compartment, the thin girl was chewing on a candy, the box open on her lap. I did not know much about the next few minutes except that all baggage was dragged down from the racks, that my baggage took longer than the baggage of my companions. I remember the heavy girl chatting away, and something being said about my traveling visa, and how I was going to a theatre festival because I was a playwright. (It was two days later before I realized I had never mentioned the Moscow theatre festival or anything about myself.) And the name Hellman came into the conversation I could only half understand. One of the customs men said, "Jew," and the heavy girl said certainly the name was not always of a Jew and gave examples of people and places I couldn't follow. Then the men thanked us, replaced everything neatly, and bowed themselves out the door.

Somewhere in the next hours I stopped being hot or cold and was not to be frightened again that day. The thin girl had neatly retied my candy box, but I don't think any of us spoke again until the train pulled into the station. When the porters came on for the baggage, I told myself that now I should be nervous, that if the money had been discovered at the border gate nothing much could have happened because I was still close to France. Now was the time, therefore, for caution, intelligence, reasonable fears. But it wasn't the time, and I laughed at that side of me that so often panics at a moment of no consequence, so often grows listless and sleepy near danger.

But there was to be no danger that day. The thin girl was right behind me on the long walk toward the station gate, people kissing and shaking hands all along the way. A man and a woman of about fifty came toward me, the woman holding out her arms and saying in English, "Lillian, how good it is to see you. How naughty of you not to stay more than a few hours, but even that will give us time for a nice visit—" as the thin girl, very close to me now, said, "Give her the candy box."

I said, "I am so glad to see you again. I have brought you a small gift, gifts—" but the box was now out of my hands and I was being moved toward the gate. Long before we reached the gate the woman and the thin girl had disappeared.

The man said, "Go through the gate. Ask the man at the gate if there is a restaurant near the station. If he says Albert's go to it. If he gives you another name, go to that one, look at it, and turn back to Albert's, which is directly opposite the door you are facing." As I asked the official at the gate about a restaurant, the man went past me. The official said please to step to one side, he was busy, would take care of me in a minute. I didn't like being in the station so I crossed the street to Albert's. I went through a revolving door and was so shocked at the sight of Julia at a table that I stopped at the door. She half rose, called softly, and I went toward her in tears that I couldn't stop because I saw two crutches lying next to her and now knew what I had never wanted to know before. Half out of her seat, holding to the table, she said, "Fine, fine. I have ordered caviar for us to celebrate. Albert had to send for it, it won't be long."

She held my hand for several minutes, and said, "Fine. Everything has gone fine. Nothing will happen now. Let's eat and drink and see each other. So many years."

"I said, "How long have we got? How far is the other station, the one where I get the train to Moscow?"

"You have two hours, but we haven't that long together because you have to be followed to the station and the ones who follow you must have time to find the man who will be with you on the train until Warsaw in the morning."

I said, "You look like nobody else. You are more beautiful now."

She said, "Stop crying about my leg. It was amputated and the false leg is clumsily made so I am coming to New York in the next few months, as soon as I can, and get a good one. Lilly, don't cry for me. *Stop the tears.* We must finish the work now. Take off the hat the way you would if it was too hot for this place. Comb your hair, and put the hat on the seat between us."

Her coat was open, and the minute I put the hat on the bench she pinned it deep inside her coat with a safety pin that was ready for it.

She said, "Now I am going to the toilet. If the waiter tries to help me up, wave him aside and come with me. The toilet locks. If anybody should try to open it, knock on the door and call to me, but I don't think that will happen."

She got up, picked up one of the crutches, and waved me to the other arm. She spoke German to a man I guess was Albert as we moved down the long room. She pulled the crutch too quickly into the toilet door, it caught at a wrong angle, and she made a gesture with the crutch, tearing at it in irritation.

When she came out of the toilet, she smiled at me. As we walked back to the table, she spoke in a loud voice, saying something in German about the toilet and then, in English, "I forget you don't know German. I was saying that German public toilets are always clean, much cleaner than ours, particularly under the new regime. The bastards, the murders."

Caviar and wine were on the table when we sat down again and she was cheerful with the waiter. When he had gone away she said, "Oh, Lilly. Fine, fine. Nothing will happen now. But it is your right to know that it is my money you brought in and we can save five hundred, and maybe, if we can bargain right, a thousand people with it. So believe that you have been better than a good friend to me, you have done something important."

"Jews?"

"About half. And political people. Socialists, Communists, plain old Catholic dissenters. Jews aren't the only people who have suffered here." She sighed. "That's enough of that. We can only do today what we can do today and today you did it for us. Do you need something stronger than wine?"

I said I didn't and she said to talk fast now, there wasn't much time, to tell her as much as possible. I told her about my divorce, about the years with Hammett. She said she had read *The Children's Hour,* she was pleased with me, and what was I going to do next?

I said, "I did it. A second play, a failure. Tell me about your baby."

"She's fat and handsome. I've got over minding that she looks like my mother."

"I want very much to see her."

"You will," she said, "I'll bring her when I come home for the new leg and she can live with you, if you like."

I said, meaning no harm, "Couldn't I see her now?"

"Are you crazy? Do you think I would bring her here? Isn't it enough I took chances with your safety? I will pay for that tonight and tomorrow and . . ." Then she smiled. "The baby lives in Mulhouse, with some nice folks. I see her that way whenever I cross the border. Maybe, when I come back for the leg, I'll leave her with you. She shouldn't be in Europe. It ain't for babies now."

"I haven't a house or even an apartment of any permanence," I said, "But I'll get one if you bring the baby."

"Sure. But it wouldn't matter. You'd be good to her." Then she laughed. "Are you as angry a woman as you were a child?"

"I think so," I said. "I try not to be, but there it is."

"Why do you try not to be?"

"If you lived around me, you wouldn't ask."

"I've always liked your anger," she said, "trusted it."

"You're the only one, then, who has."

"Don't let people talk you out of it. It may be uncomfortable for them, but it's valuable to you. It's what made you bring the money in today. Yes, I'll leave the baby with you. Its father won't disturb you, he wants nothing to do with the baby or with me. He's O.K. Just an ordinary climber. I don't know why I did it, Freud told me not to, but I don't care. The baby's good."

She smiled and patted my hand. "Someday I will take you to meet Freud. What am I saying? I will probably never see him again—I have only so much longer to last in Europe. The crutches make me too noticeable. The man who will take care of you has just come into the street. Do you see him outside the window? Get up and go now. Walk across the street, get a taxi, take it to Bahnhof 200. Another man will be waiting there. He will make sure you get safely on the train and will stay with you until Warsaw tomorrow morning. He is in car A, compartment 13. Let me see your ticket."

I gave it to her. "I think that will be in the car to your left." She laughed. "*Left*, Lilly, *left*. Have you ever learned to tell left from right, south from north?"

"No. I don't want to leave you. The train doesn't go for over an hour. I want to stay with you a few more minutes."

"No," she said. "Something could still go wrong and we must have time to get help if that should happen. I'll be coming to New York in a few months. Write from Moscow to American Express in Paris. I have stuff picked up every few weeks." She took my hand and raised it to her lips. "My beloved friend."

Then she pushed me and I was on my feet. When I got to the door I turned and must have taken a step back because she shook her head and moved her face to look at another part of the room.

I did not see the man who followed me to the station. I did not see the other man on the train, although several times a youngish man passed my compartment and the same man took the vacant chair next to me at dinner, but didn't speak to me at all.

When I went back to my compartment from dinner the conductor asked if I wanted my two small valises put in the corridor for examination when we crossed the German-Polish border so that I wouldn't be awakened. I told him I had a wardrobe trunk in the baggage car, handed him the key for the customs people, and went to sleep on the first sleeping pill of my life, which may be why I didn't wake up until just before we pulled into the Warsaw station at seven in the morning. There was bustle in the station as I raised the curtain to look out. Standing below my window was the young man who had sat next to me at dinner. He made a gesture with his hand, but I didn't understand and shook my head. Then he looked around and pointed to his right. I shook my head again, bewildered, and he moved away from the window. In a minute there was a knock on my door and I rose to open it. An English accent said through the crack, "Good morning. Wanted to say goodbye to you, have a happy trip." And then, very, very softly, "Your trunk was removed by the Germans. You are in no danger because you are across the border. Do nothing for a few hours and then ask the Polish conductor about the trunk. Don't return from Moscow through Germany, travel another way." In a loud voice he said, "My best regards to your family," and disappeared.

For two hours I sat in bed, doubtful, frightened of the next move, worried about the loss of clothes in my trunk. When I got dressed, I asked the Polish conductor if the German conductor had left my trunk key with him. He was upset when he told me the German customs people had removed the trunk, that often happened, but he was sure it would be sent on to me in Moscow after a few days, nothing unusual, the German swine often did it now.

The trunk did arrive in Moscow two weeks later. The lining was in shreds, the drawers were broken, but only a camera was missing and four or five books. I did not know then, and I do not know now, whether the trunk had anything to do with Julia because I was not to see Germany for thirty years and I was never to speak with Julia again.

I wrote to her from Moscow, again from Prague on my way back to Paris, and after I had returned to New York from Spain during the Civil War. Three or four months later I had a card with a Geneva postmark. It said, says, "Good girl to go to Spain. Did it convince you? We'll talk about that when I return to New York in March."

But March and April came and went and there was no word from Julia. I telephone her grandmother, but I should have known better. The old lady said they hadn't heard from Julia in two years and why did I keep worrying her? I said I had seen Julia in October and she hung up the phone. Somewhere about that time I saw a magazine picture of Julia's mother, who had just married again, an Argentine, but I saw no reason for remembering his name.

On May 23, 1938, I had a cable, dated London two days before and sent to the wrong address. It said, "Julia has been killed stop please advise Moore's funeral home Whitechapel Road London what disposition stop my sorrow for you for all of us." It was signed John Watson but had no address.

It is never possible for me to cry at the time when it could do me some good, so, instead, I got very drunk for two days and don't remember anything about them. The third morning I went around to Julia's grandmother's house and was told by the butler, who came out on the street as if I were a danger to the house, that the old people were on a world cruise and wouldn't be back for eight weeks. I asked the name of the boat, was asked for my credentials, and by the time we batted all that around, I was screaming that their granddaughter was dead and that he and they could go fuck themselves. I was so sick that night that Dash, who never wanted me to go anywhere because he never wanted to, said he thought I should go to London right away.

I have no diary notes of that trip and now only the memory of standing over a body with a restored face that didn't hide the knife wound that ran down the left side. The funeral man explained that he had tried to cover the face slash but I should see the wounds on the body if I wanted to see a mess that couldn't be covered. I left the place and stood on the street for a while. When I went back in the funeral man handed me a note over the lunch he was eating. The note said, "Dear Miss Hellman. We have counted on your coming but perhaps it is not possible for you, so I will send a carbon of this to your New York address. None of us knows what disposition her family wishes to make, where they want what should be a hero's funeral. It is your right to know that the Nazis found her in Frankfurt, in the apartment of a colleague. We got her to London in the hope of saving her. Sorry that I cannot be here to help you. It is better that I take my sorrow for this wonderful woman into action and perhaps revenge. Yours, John Watson, who speaks here for the many others. Salud."

I went away that day and toward evening telephoned the funeral man to ask if he had an address for John Watson. He said he had never heard the name John Watson, he had picked up the body at the house of a Dr. Chester Lowe at 30 Downshire Hill. When I got there it was a house that had been made into apartments, but there was no Dr. Lowe on the name plates, and for the first time it occurred to me that my investigations could be bad for people who were themselves in danger.

So I brought the body home with me on the old *De Grasse* and tried this time to reach Julia's mother. The same butler told me that he couldn't give me her mother's address, although he knew the mother had been informed of the death. I had the body cremated and the ashes are still where they were that day so long ago.

Karl Baedeker

BERLIN'S GENERAL ASPECT

As REGARDS ITS *General Aspect*, Berlin suffers from the dead level of its site, and also, since three-quarters of its buildings are quite modern, from a certain lack of historical interest. The Church of St. Nicholas, the Church of St. Mary, the Kloster-Kirche, and the Chapel of the Holy Ghost are practically the only buildings remaining of the old town, which consisted of narrow, crooked streets of dwelling-houses, and a few larger cloisters and hospitals grouped round the two Town Halls. With improved means of locomotion the inner town

The Baedeker name has long been synonymous with tourism. This guidebook empire was begun by Karl Baedeker (1801-1859) in Koblenz. This excerpt is from the 1912 edition of his Berlin guide.

has now gradually become the commercial nucleus of Berlin, like the City in London. Immense and palatial buildings have arisen, occupied from floor to ceiling by business-offices and ware-rooms. The approaches to the old town have been widened, new ones have been built, and the Spree has been cleared of obstructions. The neighbourhood of the *Royal Palace* has been remodelled in harmony with the baroque forms of the palace itself. The Lustgarten, the Opera House Square, and the Linden together form a broad and magnificent thoroughfare of the first rank, such as may possibly be paralleled in Vienna, but certainly not in either London or Paris. The street known as *Unter den Linden* which had hardly lived up to its ancient reputation, has again become one of the chief arteries of traffic. The old houses are disappearing, magnificent hotels and business-premises have sprung up, while the avenues of trees and the footpaths have been altered and modernized. The system on which the *Friedrichstadt,* to the S. of the Linden, is laid out, points to its origin in the mere will of the soverign. The regular streets crossing each other at right angles have not arisen from the needs of traffic; the few squares, such as the

Gendarmen-Markt, have been arbitrarily inserted. Here also, however, the old houses have been replaced by magnificent new buildings, notably in the chief streets. The Behren-Strasse, the chief residence of the diplomats down to 1870, the Mauer-Strasse and the Kanonier-Strasse, all now contain numerous banking-houses and insurance-offices. The Spittel-Markt and the Hausvogtei-Platz are commercial centres, while the invasion of the residential quarters by business-premises progresses steadily towards the W. and already extends far up in the neighbourhood of the Leipziger-Strasse.

Neither the expansion of the town in the 18th century, nor the system of building adopted in 1860, was conducive to originality or variety in the different quarters. For miles the whole ground was systematically marked out, without any great consideration of the characteristic difference between the wide main arteries and such smaller side-streets as might be found necessary. The enormous prices of the large building-lots, which were generally very narrow in proportion to their depth, necessitated the building of high houses with narrow courts. All over the town we find on the same plots expensive residences in front and cheaper and crowded ones behind, thus causing a great mixture of all classes of the inhabitants, and great monotony of street effects. It is only within recent years that some of the suburbs have been laid out on the villa-system.

Just as in London, in Paris, and other capitals, so in Berlin, the upper classes tend on the whole to live at the W. end of the town, while the E. end is given over to factories and workshops. The *South-Eastern Quarter* is the seat of the more skilled industries, such as cabinet-making and the manufacture of articles in bronze and other metals. The place of the old building-yards and factories is gradually being taken by the so-called *Höfe,* huge, many-storied buildings, often enclosing three or four interior courts, and airy and well lighted from floor to ceiling, while the motive power for the machinery is furnished by steam or electricity. Similar erections serve as warehouses for industrial samples. Several imposing buildings, such as hospitals and churches, are to be seen more towards the centre of the town, and large barracks are found in the S. quarters, near the large parade-ground on the Tempelhofer Feld, the W. half of which was recently detached as building-ground. Adjacent to the E. is *Neukölln* (formerly Rixdorf), which in the last decades has developed into a town of considerable dimensions.—The NORTH-EASTERN QUARTER is the seat of the woollen and clothing industries, and contains little that is worth seeing. The Friedrichshain, however, forms a pleasant oasis here. Farther out is the Central Slaughter House.

The NORTHERN QUARTER was from 1860 to 1880 the seat of great machine-works and foundries. Since then the manufactories have been transferrred to the N.W. as far as the neighbourhood of Tegel, and the buildings containing the Physical Science Schools and their collections now stand on the site of the old royal iron-foundry. In the extreme N. are the suburbs of *Pankow* and *Nieder-Schönhausen*. —The NORTH-WEST QUARTER is being given over more and more to barracks, courts-of-law, medical institutes, and hospitals. The district of *Moabit* is surrounded by them, while the *Hansa Quarter*, which lies beyond the Spree and adjoins the park of Schloss Bellevue, can boast of several streets of high-class residences.

THE WESTERN QUARTER is the favourite abode of the well-to-do inhabitants on account of its proximity to the Tiergarten. In place of the large park and small villas which once surrounded the woods, the aristocratic *Tiergarten Quarter* has arisen since 1850, with its handsome villas, gardens, and private roads, stretching on to the S. to the Landwehr Canal and on the W. to the Zoological Garden. The gardens, however, are gradually disappearing before the encroachments of bricks and mortar, the ground to the S. of the canal being almost entirely built over. In the *Potsdamer-Strasse* the business life of the Leipziger-Strasse extends as far as Schöneberg. The *Kurfürsten-Damm,* a magnificent street beginning on the S. side of the Zoological Garden, runs to the S.W. to the Grunewald. The surroundings of the *Grunewald,* which marches with *Halensee,* are given over to villas. To the N. the W. end of Berlin borders on *Charlottenburg,* to the S. on *Schöneberg* and *Wilmersdorf,* the space once intervening between the city and these suburbs being now entirely built over. The outlying suburbs on the Wannsee Railway, *Friedenau, Steglitz,* and *Lichterfelde* are also rapidly rising in extent and importance, and *Dahlem* will follow them if other scientific institutions be transferred there.

Almost every part of Berlin offers a pleasing picture. Its streets are a model of cleanliness, while a system of main drainage, radiating in twelve directions, carries all of its sewage to distant fields. There are few dark lanes or alleys even in the old part of the city. Nearly all the newer houses have balconies, gay in summer with flowers and foliage. The public squares are embellished with gardens, monuments, and fountains, and the newer churches also are generally surrounded by small pleasure-grounds. Numerous bridges are beautified with sculpture. The centres of traffic, such as the Jannowitz-Brücke, the Trebbiner-Strasse, the Lehrte Station, etc., with their network of railway-lines, and the navigation on the river offer scenes of remarkable animation.

Christopher Isherwood

A BERLIN DIARY

(WINTER 1932–3)

TONIGHT, FOR THE first time this winter, it is very cold. The dead cold grips the town in utter silence, like the silence of intense midday summer heat. In the cold the town seems actually to contract, to dwindle to a small black dot, scarcely larger than hundreds of other dots, isolated and hard to find, on the enormous European map. Outside, in the night, beyond the last new-built blocks of concrete flats, where the streets end in frozen allotment gardens, are the

Christopher Isherwood was born in England in 1904 and lived in Berlin from 1929 to 1933. Along with Spender and Auden, Isherwood documented pre-Nazi Berlin in writings such as this excerpt from Goodbye to Berlin.

Prussian plains. You can feel them all round you, tonight, creeping in upon the city, like an immense waste of unhomely ocean—sprinkled with leafless copses and ice-lakes and tiny villages which are remembered only as the outlandish names of battlefields in half-forgotten wars. Berlin is a skeleton which aches in the cold: it is my own skeleton aching. I feel in my bones the sharp ache of the frost in the girders of the overhead railway, in the ironwork of balconies, in bridges, tramlines, lamp-standards, latrines. The iron throbs and shrinks, the stone and the bricks ache dully, the plaster is numb.

Berlin is a city with two centres—the cluster of expensive hotels, bars, cinemas, shops round the Memorial Church, a sparkling nucleus of light, like a sham diamond, in the shabby twilight of the town; and the self-conscious civic centre of buildings round the Unter den Linden, carefully arranged. In grand international styles, copies of copies, they assert our dignity as a capital city—a parliament, a couple of museums, a State bank, a cathedral, an opera, a dozen embassies, a triumphal arch; nothing has been forgotten. And they are all so pompous, so very correct—all except the cathedral, which betrays, in its architecture, a flash of that hysteria which flickers always behind every grave, grey Prussian façade. Extinguished by its absurd dome, it is, at first sight, so startlingly funny that one searches for a name suitably preposterous—the Church of the Immaculate Consumption.

But the real heart of Berlin is a small damp black wood—the Tiergarten. At this time of the year, the cold begins to drive the peasant boys out of their tiny unprotected villages into the city, to look for food, and work. But the city, which glowed so brightly and invitingly in the night sky above the plains, is cold and cruel and dead. Its warmth is an illusion, a mirage of the winter desert. It will not receive these boys. It has nothing to give. The cold drives them out of its streets, into the wood which is its cruel heart. And there they cower on benches, to starve and freeze, and dream of their far-away cottage stoves.

HERR KRAMPF, A young engineer, one of my pupils, describes his childhood during the days of the War and the Inflation. During the last years of the War, the straps disappeared from the windows of railway carriages: people had cut them off in order to sell the leather. You even saw men and women going about in clothes made from the carriage upholstery. A party of Krampf's school friends broke into a factory one night and stole all the leather driving-belts. Everybody stole. Everybody sold what they had to sell—themselves included. A boy of fourteen, from Krampf's class, peddled cocaine between school hours, in the streets.

Farmers and butchers were omnipotent. Their slightest whim had to be gratified, if you wanted vegetables or meat. The Krampf family knew of a butcher in a little village outside Berlin who always had meat to sell. But the butcher had a peculiar sexual perversion. His greatest erotic pleasure was to pinch and slap the cheeks of a sensitive, well-bred girl or woman. The possibility of thus humiliating a lady like Frau Krampf excited him enormously: unless he was allowed to realize his fantasy, he refused, absolutely, to do business. So, every Sunday, Krampf's mother would travel out to the village with her children, and patiently offer her cheeks to be slapped and pinched, in exchange for some cutlets or a steak.

AT THE FAR end of the Potsdamerstrasse, there is a fair-ground, with merry-go-rounds, swings and peep-shows. One of the chief attractions of the fair-ground is a tent where boxing and wrestling matches are held. You pay your money and go in, the wrestlers fight three or four rounds, and the referee then announces that, if you want to see any more, you must pay an extra ten pfennigs. One of the wrestlers is a bald man with a very large stomach: he wears a pair of canvas trousers rolled up at the bottoms, as though he were going paddling. His opponent wears black tights, and leather kneelets which look as if they had come off an old cab-horse. The wrestlers throw each other about as much as possible, turning somersaults in the air to amuse the audience. The fat man who plays the part of the loser pretends to get very angry when he is beaten, and threatens to fight the referee.

One of the boxers is a negro. He invariably wins. The boxers hit each other with the open glove, making a tremendous amount of noise. The other boxer, a tall, well-built young man, about twenty years younger and obviously much stronger than the negro, is "knocked out" with absurd ease. He writhes in great agony on the floor, nearly manages to struggle to his feet at the count of ten, then collapses again, groaning. After this fight, the referee collects ten more pfennigs and calls for a challenger from the audience. Before any bona fide challenger can apply, another young man, who has been quite openly chatting and joking with the wrestlers, jumps hastily into the ring and strips off his clothes, revealing himself already dressed in shorts and boxer's boots. The referee announces a purse of five marks; and, this time, the negro is "knocked out."

The audience took the fights dead seriously, shouting encouragement to the fighters, and even quarrelling and betting amongst themselves on the results. Yet nearly all of them had been in the tent as long as I had, and stayed on after I had left. The political moral is certainly depressing: these people could be made to believe in anybody or anything.

WALKING THIS EVENING along the Kleiststrasse, I saw a little crowd gathered round a private car. In the car were two girls: on the pavement stood two young Jews, engaged in a violent argument with a large blond man who was obviously rather drunk. The Jews, it seemed, had been driving slowly along the street, on the look-out for a pick-up, and had offered these girls a ride. The two girls had accepted and got into the car. At this moment, however, the blond man had intervened. He was a Nazi, he told us, and as such felt it his mission to defend the honor of all German women against the obscene anti-Nordic menace. The two Jews didn't seem in the least intimidated; they told the Nazi energetically to mind his own business. Meanwhile, the girls, taking advantage of the row, slipped out of the car and ran off down the street. The Nazi then tried to drag one of the Jews with him to find a policeman, and the Jew whose arm he had seized gave him an uppercut which laid him sprawling on his back.

Before the Nazi could get to his feet, both young men had jumped into their car and driven away. The crowd dispersed slowly, arguing. Very few of them sided openly with the Nazi: several supported the Jews; but the majority confined themselves to shaking their heads dubiously and murmuring: *"Allerhand!"*

When, three hours later, I passed the same spot, the Nazi was still patrolling up and down, looking hungrily for more German womanhood to rescue.

WE HAVE JUST got a letter from Frl. Mayr: Frl. Schroeder called me in to listen to it. Frl. Mayr doesn't like Holland. She has been obliged to sing in a lot of second-rate cafés in third-rate towns, and her bedroom is often badly heated. The Dutch, she writes, have no culture; she has only met one truly refined and superior gentleman, a widower. The widowers tells her that she is a really womanly woman—he has no use for young chits of girls. He has shown his admiration for her art presenting her with a complete new set of underclothes.

Frl. Mayr has also had trouble with her colleagues. At one town, a rival actress, jealous of Frl. Mayr's vocal powers, tried to stab her in the eye with a hat-pin. I can't help admiring that actress's courage. When Frl. Mayr had finished with her, she was so badly injured that she couldn't appear on the stage again for a week.

LAST NIGHT, FRITZ Wendel proposed a tour of "the dives." It was to be in the nature of a farewell visit, for the Police have begun to take a great interest in these places. They are frequently raided, and the names of their clients are written down. There is even talk of a general Berlin clean-up.

I rather upset him by insisting on visiting the Salomé, which I had never seen. Fritz, as a connoisseur of night-life, was most contemptuous. It wasn't even genuine, he told me. The management run it entirely for the benefit of provincial sightseers.

The Salomé turned out to be very expensive and even more depressing than I had imagined. A few stage lesbians and some young men with plucked eyebrows lounged at the bar, uttering occasional raucous guffaws or treble hoots—supposed, apparently, to represent the laughter of the damned. The whole premises are painted gold and inferno-red—crimson plush inches thick, and vast gilded mirrors. It was pretty full. The audience consisted chiefly of respectable middle-aged tradesmen and their families, exclaiming in good-humored amazement: "Do they really?" and "Well, I never!" We went out half-way through the cabaret performance, after a young man in a spangled crinoline and jewelled breast-caps had painfully but successfully executed three splits.

At the entrance we met a party of American youths, very drunk, wondering whether to go in. Their leader was a small stocky young man in pince-nez, with an annoyingly prominent jaw.

"Say," he asked Fritz, "what's on here?"

"Men dressed as women," Fritz grinned.

The little American simply couldn't believe it. "Men dressed as *women?* As *women* hey? Do you mean they're *queer?*"

"Eventually we're all queer," drawled Fritz solemnly, in lugubrious tones. The young man looked us over slowly. He had been running and was still out of breath. The others grouped themselves awkwardly behind him, ready for anything—though their callow, open-mouthed faces in the greenish lamp-light looked a bit scared.

"You *queer*, too, hey?" demanded the little American, turning suddenly on me.

"Yes," I said, "very queer indeed."

He stood before me a moment, panting, thrusting out his jaw, uncertain it seemed, whether he ought not to hit me in the face. Then he turned, uttered some kind of wild college battle-cry, and, followed by the others, rushed headlong into the building.

"EVER BEEN TO that communist dive near the Zoo?" Fritz asked me, as we were walking away from the Salomé. "Eventually we should cast an eye in there. . . . In six months, maybe, we'll all be wearing red shirts. . . ."

I agreed. I was curious to know what Fritz's idea of

a "communist dive" would be like.

It was, in fact, a small whitewashed cellar. You sat on long wooden benches at big bare tables; a dozen people together—like a school dining-hall. On the walls were scribbled expressionist drawings involving actual newspaper clippings, real playing-cards, nailed-on beer-mats, match-boxes, cigarette cartons, and heads cut out of photographs. The café was full of students, dressed mostly with aggressive political untidiness—the men in sailor's sweaters and stained baggy trousers, the girls in ill-fitting jumpers, skirts held visibly together with safety-pins and carelessly knotted gaudy gypsy scarves. The proprietress was smoking a cigar. The boy who acted as a waiter lounged about with a cigarette between his lips and slapped customers on the back when taking their orders.

It was all thoroughly sham and gay and jolly: you couldn't help feeling at home, immediately. Fritz, as usual, recognized plenty of friends. He introduced me to three of them—a man called Martin, an art student named Werner, and Inge, his girl. Inge was broad and lively—she wore a little hat with a feather in it which gave her a kind of farcical resemblance to Henry the Eighth. While Werner and Inge chattered, Martin sat silent: he was thin and dark and hatchet-faced, with the sardonically superior smile of the conscious conspirator. Later in the evening, when Fritz and Werner and Inge had moved down the table to join another party, Martin began to talk about the coming civil war. When the war breaks out, Martin explained, the communists, who have very few machine-guns, will get command of the roof tops. They will then keep the Police at bay with hand-grenades. It will only be necessary to hold out for three days, because the Soviet fleet will make an immediate dash for Swinemünde and begin to land troops. "I spend most of my time now making bombs," Martin added. I nodded and grinned, very much embarrassed—uncertain whether he was making fun of me, or deliberately committing some appalling indiscretion. He certainly wasn't drunk, and he didn't strike me as merely insane.

Presently, a strikingly handsome boy of sixteen or seventeen came into the café. His name was Rudi. He was dressed in a Russian blouse, leather shorts and despatch-rider's boots, and he strode up to our table with all the heroic mannerisms of a messenger who returns successful from a desperate mission. He had, however, no message of any kind to deliver. After his whirlwind entry, and a succession of curt, martial handshakes, he sat down quite quietly beside us and ordered a glass of tea.

THIS EVENING, I visited the "communist" café again. It is really a fascinating little world of intrigue and counter-intrigue. Its Napoleon is the sinister bomb-making Martin; Werner is its Danton; Rudi its Joan of Arc. Everybody suspects everybody else. Already Martin has warned me against Werner: he is "politically unreliable"—last summer he stole the entire funds of a communist youth organization. And Werner has warned me against Martin: he is either a Nazi agent, or a police spy, or in the pay of the French Government. In addition to this, both Martin and Werner earnestly advised me to have nothing to do with Rudi—they absolutely refused to say why.

But there was no question of having nothing to do with Rudi. He planted himself down beside me and began talking at once—a hurricane of enthusiasm. His favourite word is "knorke": "Oh, *ripping!*" He is a pathfinder. He wanted to know what the boy scouts were like in England. Had they got the spirit of adventure? "All German boys are adventurous. Adventure is ripping. Our Scoutmaster is a ripping man. Last year he went to Lapland and lived in a hut, all through the summer, alone. . . . Are you a communist?"

"No. Are you?"

Rudi was pained.

"Of course! We all are, here. . . . I'll lend you some books, if you like. . . . You ought to come and see our clubhouse. It's ripping. . . . We sing the Red Flag, and all the forbidden songs. . . . Will you teach me English? I want to learn all languages."

I asked if there were any girls in his pathfinder group. Rudi was as shocked as if I'd said something really indecent.

"Women are no good," he told me bitterly. "They spoil everything. They haven't got the spirit of adventure. Men understand each other much better when they're alone together. Uncle Peter (that's our Scoutmaster) says women should stay at home and mend socks. That's all they're fit for!"

"Is Uncle Peter a communist, too?"

"Of course!" Rudi looked at me suspiciously. "Why do you ask that?"

"Oh, no special reason," I replied hastily. "I think perhaps I was mixing him up with somebody else. . . . "

THIS AFTERNOON I travelled out to the reformatory to visit one of my pupils, Herr Brink, who is a master there. He is a small, broad-shouldered man, with the thin, dead-looking fair hair, mild eyes, and bulging, over-heavy forehead of the German vegetarian intellectual. He wears sandals and an open-necked shirt. I found him in the gymnasium, giving physical instruction to a class of mentally deficient children—for the reformatory houses mental deficients as well as juvenile delinquents. With a certain melancholy pride, he pointed out the various cases: one little boy was suffering from hereditary syphilis—he had a fearful squint; another, the child of elderly drunkards, couldn't stop laughing. They clambered about the wall-bars like monkeys, laughing and chattering, seemingly quite happy.

Then we went up to the workshop, where older boys in blue overalls—all convicted criminals—were making boots. Most of the boys looked up and grinned when Brink came in, only a few were sullen. But I couldn't look them in the eyes. I felt horribly guilty and ashamed: I seemed, at that moment, to have become the sole representative of their gaolers, of Capitalist Society. I wondered if any of them had actually been arrested in the Alexander Casino, and, if so, whether they recognized me.

We had lunch in the matron's room. Herr Brink apologized for giving me the same food as the boys themselves ate—potato soup with two sausages, and a dish of apples and stewed prunes. I protested—as, no doubt, I was intended to protest—that it was very good. And yet the thought of the boys having to eat it, or any other kind of meal, in that building made each spoonful stick in my throat. Institutional food has an indescribable, perhaps

purely imaginary, taste. (One of the most vivid and sickening memories of my own school life, is the smell of ordinary
white bread.)

"You don't have any bars or locked gates here," I
said. "I thought all reformatories had them. . . . Don't your
boys often run away?"

"Hardly ever," said Brink, and the admission
seemed to make him positively unhappy; he sank his head
wearily in his hands. "Where shall they run to? Here it is
bad. At home it is worse. The majority of them know that."

"But isn't there a kind of natural instinct for freedom?"

"Yes, you are right. But the boys soon lose it. The
system helps them to lose it. I think perhaps that, in Germans, this instinct is never very strong."

"You don't have much trouble here, then?"

"Oh, yes. Sometimes. . . . Three months ago, a terrible thing happened. One boy stole another boy's overcoat.
He asked for permission to go into the town—that is
allowed—and possibly he meant to sell it. But the owner of
the coat followed him, and they had a fight. The boy to

whom the overcoat belonged took up a big stone and flung it at the other boy; and this boy, feeling himself hurt, deliberately smeared dirt into the wound, hoping to make it worse and so escape punishment. The wound did get worse. In three days the boy died of blood-poisoning. And when the other boy heard of this he killed himself with a kitchen knife. . . ." Brink sighed deeply: "Sometimes I almost despair," he added. "It seems as if there were a kind of badness, a disease, infecting the world to-day."

"But what can you really do for these boys?" I asked.

"Very little. We teach them a trade. Later, we try to find them work—which is almost impossible. If they have work in the neighbourhood, they can still sleep here at nights. . . . The Principal believes that their lives can be changed through the teachings of the Christian religion. I'm afraid I cannot feel this. The problem is not so simple. I'm afraid that most of them, if they cannot get work, will take to crime. After all, people cannot be ordered to starve."

"Isn't there any alternative?"

Brink rose and led me to the window.

"You see those two buildings? One is the engineering-works, the other is the prison. For the boys of this district there used to be two alternatives. . . . But now the works are bankrupt. Next week they will close down."

THIS MORNING I went to see Rudi's club-house, which is also the office of a pathfinders' magazine. The editor and scoutmaster, Uncle Peter, is a haggard, youngish man, with a parchment-coloured face and deeply sunken eyes, dressed in corduroy jacket and shorts. He is evidently Rudi's idol. The only time Rudi will stop talking is when Uncle Peter has something to say. They showed me dozens of photographs of boys, all taken with the camera tilted upwards, from beneath, so that they look like epic giants, in profile against enormous clouds. The magazine itself has articles on hunting, tracking, and preparing food—all written in super-enthusiastic style, with a curious underlying note of hysteria, as though the actions described were part of a religious or erotic ritual. There were half-a-dozen other boys in the room with us: all of them in a state of heroic semi-nudity, wearing the shortest of shorts and the thinnest of shirts or singlets, although the weather is so cold.

When I had finished looking at the photographs, Rudi took me into the club meeting-room. Long coloured banners hung down the walls, embroidered with initials and mysterious totem devices. At one end of the room was a low table covered with a crimson embroidered cloth—a kind of altar. On the table were candles in brass candlesticks.

"We light them on Thursdays," Rudi explained, "when we have our camp-fire palaver. Then we sit round in a ring on the floor, and sing songs and tell stories."

Above the table with the candlesticks was a sort of icon—the framed drawing of a young pathfinder of unearthly beauty, gazing sternly into the far distance, a banner in his hand. The whole place made me feel profoundly uncomfortable. I excused myself and got away as soon as I could.

OVERHEARD IN A café: a young Nazi is sitting with his girl; they are discussing the future of the Party. The Nazi is drunk.

"Oh, I know we shall win, all right," he exclaims impatiently, "but that's not enough!" He thumps the table with his fist: "Blood must flow!"

The girl strokes his arm reassuringly. She is trying to get him to come home. "But, *of course*, it's going to flow, darling," she coos soothingly, "the Leader's promised that in our programme."

TO-DAY IS "Silver Sunday." The streets are crowded with shoppers. All along the Tauentzienstrasse, men, women and boys are hawking post-cards, flowers, song-books, hair-oil, bracelets. Christmas-trees are stacked for sale along the central path between the tram-lines. Uniformed S.A. men rattle their collecting-boxes. In the side-streets, lorry-loads of police are waiting; for any large crowd, nowadays, is capable of turning into a political riot. The Salvation Army have a big illuminated tree on the Wittenbergplatz, with a blue electric star. A group of students were standing round it, making sarcastic remarks. Among them I recognized Werner, from the "communist" café.

"This time next year," said Werner, "that star will have changed its colour!" He laughed violently—he was in an excited, slightly hysterical mood. Yesterday, he told me, he'd had a great adventure: "You see, three other comrades and myself decided to make a demonstration at the Labour Exchange in Neukölln. I had to speak, and the others were to see I wasn't interrupted. We went round there at about half-past ten, when the bureau's most crowded. Of course, we'd planned it all beforehand—each of the comrades had to hold one of the doors, so that none of the clerks in the office could get out. There they were, cooped up like rabbits. . . . Of course, we couldn't prevent their telephoning for the Police, we knew that. We reckoned we'd got six or seven minutes. . . . Well, as soon as the doors were fixed, I jumped on to a table. I just yelled whatever came into my head—I don't know what I said. They liked it, anyhow. . . . In half a minute I had them so excited I got quite scared. I was afraid they'd break into the office and lynch somebody. There was a fine old shindy, I can tell you! But just when things were beginning to look properly lively, a comrade came up from below to tell us the Police were there already—just getting out of their car. So we had to make a dash for it. . . . I think they'd have got us, only the crowd was on our side, and wouldn't let them through until we were out by the other door, into the street. . . ." Werner finished breathlessly, "I tell you, Christopher," he added, "the capitalist system can't possibly last much longer now. The workers are on the move!"

EARLY THIS EVENING I was in the Bülowstrasse. There had been a big Nazi meeting at the Sportpalast, and groups of men and boys were just coming away from it, in their brown or black uniforms. Walking along the pavement ahead of me were three S.A. men. They all carried Nazi banners on their shoulders, like rifles, rolled tight round the staves—the banner-staves had sharp metal points, shaped into arrow-heads.

All at once, the three S.A. men came face to face with a youth of seventeen or eighteen, dressed in civilian clothes, who was hurrying along in the opposite direction. I heard one of the Nazis shout: "That's him!" and immediately all three of them flung themselves upon the young man. He uttered a scream, and tried to dodge, but they were too quick for him. In a moment they had jostled him into the shadow of a house entrance, and were standing over him, kicking him and stabbing at him with the sharp metal points of their banners. All this happened with such incredible speed that I could hardly believe my eyes—already, the three S.A. men had left their victim, and were barging their way through the crowd; they made for the stairs which led up to the station of the Overhead Railway.

Another passer-by and myself were the first to reach the doorway where the young man was lying. He lay huddled crookedly in the corner, like an abandoned sack. As they picked him up, I got a sickening glimpse of his face—his left eye was poked half out, and blood poured from the wound. He wasn't dead. Somebody volunteered to take him to the hospital in a taxi.

By this time, dozens of people were looking on. They seemed surprised, but not particularly shocked—this sort of thing happened too often, nowadays. "*Allerhand....*" they murmured. Twenty yards away, at the Potsdamerstrasse corner, stood a group of heavily armed policemen. With their chests out, and their hands on their revolver belts, they magnificently disregarded the whole affair.

WERNER HAS BECOME a hero. His photograph was in the *Rote Fahne* a few days ago, captioned: "Another victim of the Police blood-bath." Yesterday, which was New Year's day, I went to visit him in the hospital.

Just after Christmas, it seems, there was a street-fight near the Stettiner Bahnhof. Werner was on the edge of the crowd, not knowing what the fight was about. On the off-chance that it might be something political, he began yelling: "Red Front!" A policeman tried to arrest him. Werner kicked the policeman in the stomach. The policeman drew his revolver and shot Werner three times through the leg. When he had finished shooting, he called another policeman, and together they carried Werner into a taxi. On the way to the police-station, the policemen hit him on the head with their truncheons, until he fainted. When he has sufficiently recovered, he will, most probably, be prosecuted.

He told me all this with the greatest satisfaction, sitting up in bed surrounded by his admiring friends, including Rudi and Inge, in her Henry the Eighth hat. Around him, on the blanket, lay his press-cuttings. Somebody had carefully underlined each mention of Werner's name with a red pencil.

TO-DAY, JANUARY 22ND, the Nazis held a demonstration on the Bülowplatz, in front of the Karl Liebknecht House. For the last week the communists have been trying to get the demonstration forbidden: they say it is simply intended as a provocation—as, of course, it was. I went along to watch it with Frank, the newspaper correspondent.

As Frank himself said afterwards, this wasn't really a Nazi demonstration at all, but a Police demonstration—there were at least two policemen to every Nazi present. Perhaps General Schleicher only allowed the march to take place in order to show who are the real masters of Berlin. Everybody says he's going to proclaim a military dictatorship.

But the real masters of Berlin are not the Police, or the Army, and certainly not the Nazis. The masters of Berlin are the workers—despite all the propaganda I've heard and read, all the demonstrations I've attended, I only realized this, for the first time to-day. Comparatively few of the hundreds of people in the streets round the Bülowplatz can have been organized communists, yet you had the feeling that every single one of them was united against this march. Somebody began to sing the "International," and, in a moment, everyone had joined in—even the women with their babies, watching from top-storey windows. The Nazis slunk past, marching as fast as they knew how, between their double rows of protectors. Most of them kept their eyes on the ground, or glared glassily ahead: a few attempted sickly, furtive grins. When the procession had passed, an elderly fat little S.A. man, who had somehow got left behind, came panting along at the double, desperately scared at finding himself alone, and trying vainly to catch up with the rest. The whole crowd roared with laughter.

During the demonstration nobody was allowed on the Bülowplatz itself. So the crowd surged uneasily about, and things began to look nasty. The police, brandishing their rifles, ordered us back; some of the less experienced ones, getting rattled, made as if to shoot. Then an armoured car appeared, and started to turn its machine-gun slowly in our direction. There was a stampede into house doorways and cafés; but no sooner had the car moved on, than everybody rushed out into the street again, shouting and singing. It was too much like a naughty schoolboy's game to be seriously alarming. Frank enjoyed himself enormously, grinning from ear to ear, and hopping about, in his flapping overcoat and huge owlish spectacles, like a mocking, ungainly bird.

ONLY A WEEK since I wrote the above. Schleicher has resigned. The monocles did their stuff. Hitler has formed a cabinet with Hugenberg. Nobody thinks it can last till the spring.

THE NEWSPAPERS ARE becoming more and more like copies of a school magazine. There is nothing in them but new rules, new punishments, and lists of people who have been "kept in." This morning, Göring has invented three fresh varieties of high treason.

Every evening, I sit in the big half-empty artists' café by the Memorial Church, where the Jews and left-wing intellectuals bend their heads together over the marble tables, speaking in low, scared voices. Many of them know that they will certainly be arrested—if not to-day, then to-morrow or next week. So they are polite and mild with each other, and raise their hats and enquire after their colleagues' families. Notorious literary tiffs of several years' standing are forgotten.

Almost every evening, the S.A. men come into the café. Sometimes they are only collecting money; everybody is compelled to give something. Sometimes they have come to make an arrest. One evening a Jewish writer, who was present, ran into the telephone-box to ring up the Police. The Nazis dragged him out, and he was taken away.

Nobody moved a finger. You could have heard a pin drop, till they were gone.

The foreign newspaper correspondents dine every night at the same little Italian restaurant, at a big round table, in the corner. Everybody else in the restaurant is watching them and trying to overhear what they are saying. If you have a piece of news to bring them—the details of an arrest, or the address of a victim whose relatives might be interviewed—then one of the journalists leaves the table and walks up and down with you outside, in the street.

A young communist I know was arrested by the S.A. men, taken to a Nazi barracks, and badly knocked about. After three or four days, he was released and went home. Next morning there was a knock at the door. The communist hobbled over to open it, his arm in a sling—and there stood a Nazi with a collecting-box. At the sight of him the communist completely lost his temper. "Isn't it enough," he yelled, "that you beat me up? And you dare to come and ask me for money?"

But the Nazi only grinned. "Now, now, comrade! No political squabbling! Remember, we're living in the

Third Reich! We're all brothers! You must try and drive that silly political hatred from your heart!"

THIS EVENING I went into the Russia tea-shop in the Kleistrasse, and there was D. For a moment I really thought I must be dreaming. He greeted me quite as usual, beaming all over his face.

"Good God!" I whispered. "What on earth are you doing here?"

D. beamed. "You thought I might have gone abroad?"

"Well, naturally. . . ."

"But the situation nowadays is so interesting. . . ."

I laughed. "That's one way of looking at it, certainly. . . . But isn't it awfully dangerous for you?"

D. merely smiled. Then he turned to the girl he was sitting with and said, "This is Mr. Isherwood. . . . You can speak quite openly to him. He hates the Nazis as much as we do. Oh yes! Mr. Isherwood is a confirmed anti-fascist!"

He laughed very heartily and slapped me on the

back. Several people who were sitting near us overheard him. Their reactions were curious. Either they simply couldn't believe their ears, or they were so scared that they pretended to hear nothing, and went on sipping their tea in a state of deaf horror. I have seldom felt so uncomfortable in my whole life.

(D's technique appears to have had its points, all the same. He was never arrested. Two months later, he successfully crossed the frontier into Holland.)

THIS MORNING, AS I was walking down the Bülow-strasse, the Nazis were raiding the house of a small liberal pacifist publisher. They had brought a lorry and were piling it with the publisher's books. The driver of the lorry mockingly read out the titles of the books to the crowd:

"*Nie Wieder Krieg!*" he shouted, holding up one of them by the corner of the cover, disgustedly, as though it were a nasty kind of reptile. Everybody roared with laughter.

"'No More War!'" echoed a fat, well-dressed woman, with a scornful, savage laugh. "What an idea!"

AT PRESENT, ONE of my regular pupils is Herr N., a police chief under the Weimar régime. He comes to me every day. He wants to brush up his English, for he is leaving very soon to take up a job in the United States. The curious thing about these lessons is that they are all given while we are driving about the streets in Herr N.'s enormous closed car. Herr N. himself never comes into our house: he sends up his chauffeur to fetch me, and the car moves off at once. Sometimes we stop for a few minutes at the edge of the Tiergarten, and stroll up and down the paths—the chauffeur always following us at a respectful distance.

Herr N. talks to me chiefly about his family. He is worried about his son, who is very delicate, and whom he is obliged to leave behind, to undergo an operation. His wife is delicate, too. He hopes the journey won't tire her. He describes her symptoms, and the kind of medicine she is taking. He tells me stories about his son as a little boy. In a tactful, impersonal way we have become quite intimate. Herr N. is always charmingly polite, and listens gravely and carefully to my explanations of grammatical points. Behind everything he says I am aware of an immense sadness.

We never discuss politics; but I know that Herr N. must be an enemy of the Nazis, and, perhaps, even in hourly danger of arrest. One morning, when we were driving along the Unter den Linden, we passed a group of self-important S.A. men, chatting to each other and blocking the whole pavement. Passers-by were obliged to walk in the gutter. Herr N. smiled faintly and sadly: "One sees some queer sights in the streets nowadays." That was his only comment.

Sometimes he will bend forward to the window and regard a building or a square with a mournful fixity, as if to impress its image upon his memory and to bid it good-bye.

TO-MORROW I AM going to England. In a few weeks I shall return, but only to pick up my things, before leaving Berlin altogether.

Poor Frl. Schroeder is inconsolable: "I shall never find another gentleman like you, Herr Issyvoo—always so punctual with the rent. . . . I'm sure I don't know what makes you want to leave Berlin, all of a sudden, like this. . . ."

It's no use trying to explain to her, or talking politics. Already she is adapting herself, as she will adapt herself to every new régime. This morning I even heard her talking reverently about "Der Führer" to the porter's wife. If anybody were to remind her that, at the elections last November, she voted communist, she would probably deny it hotly, and in perfect good faith. She is merely acclimatizing herself, in accordance with a natural law, like an animal which changes its coat for the winter. Thousands of people like Frl. Schroeder are acclimatizing themselves. After all, whatever government is in power, they are doomed to live in this town.

TO-DAY THE SUN is brilliantly shining; it is quite mild and warm. I go out for my last morning walk, without an overcoat or hat. The sun shines, and Hitler is master of this city. The sun shines, and dozens of my friends—my pupils at the Workers' School, the men and women I met at the I.A.H.—are in prison, possibly dead. But it isn't of them that I am thinking—the clear-headed ones, the purposeful, the heroic; they recognized and accepted the risks. I am thinking of poor Rudi, in his absurd Russian blouse. Rudi's make-believe, story-book game has become earnest; the Nazis will play it with him. The Nazis won't laugh at him; they'll take him on trust for what he pretended to be. Perhaps at this very moment Rudi is being tortured to death.

I catch sight of my face in the mirror of a shop, and am horrified to see that I am smiling. You can't help smiling, in such beautiful weather. The trams are going up and down the Kleiststrasse, just as usual. They, and the people on the pavement, and the teacosy dome of the Nollendorfplatz station have an air of curious familiarity, of striking resemblance to something one remembers as normal and pleasant in the past—like a very good photograph.

No. Even now I can't altogether believe that any of this has really happened. . . .

Josephine Baker

FROM BERLIN TO THE FOLIES-BERGÈRE

BERLIN. I FOUND it dazzling. The city had a jewel-like sparkle, especially at night, that didn't exist in Paris. The vast cafés reminded me of ocean liners powered by the rhythms of their orchestras. There was music everywhere. Word of our success at the Champs-Élysées had preceded us and we were greeted with great excitement. There were rumors that the show was indecent, an impression I may have strengthened when a reporter asked me to describe my ideal world. One where we can all go naked, as in paradise, I

One of the most famous entertainers of her day, Josephine Baker's Revue Négre took the world by storm. Her death in 1975 was cause for national mourning in her adopted home of France.

replied. I was quick to add that few of us can *afford* to show our bodies.

I was immediately caught up in a whirlwind of flowers, declarations of love, new acquaintances. One night I was told that the most famous director in Germany was in the audience. I was used to such descriptions by now. Everyone I met seemed to be "the greatest," "the most eminent," "the finest." Perhaps this was sometimes the case, but in my ignorance how was I to know? Fame is a ladder with many rungs and there is one for each of us. Back in St. Louis, everyone knew Mrs. Nichols's cat because one of its ears had been ripped off by a dog! When I politely murmured, "Everyone says you're the most famous painter [writer/journalist; the most beautiful woman] in Berlin," my listener's face would glisten like a flower after the rain. But I quickly realized that the description "famous director" was more than idle chatter. The intensity of his gaze was like banked fire: he glowed with an inner light. It appeared that Max Reinhardt was immensely creative, interested in all forms of theater and completely unconventional. He had staged superb tragedy in a circus and believed that theater was for everyone. Before I could begin my "Everyone says you're . . ." he informed me, through an interpreter, that I had tremendous presence and that the only thing that really interested him on the stage was an actor's personality. The finest scenery and lighting were mere window dressing for the performer who gave a show its flesh and blood. That was why he liked the *Revue Nègre* and admired my work. I seemed oblivious to rules. . . . He appeared to sense my feelings and what I was trying to do. No one had ever spoken to me about the theater that way before. "I'd like you to stay here and work with me at the Deutsche Theater," he announced. "With a few years' study, you could become a fine comedienne." My eyes filled with tears. "I can't," I stammered. "I've signed a contract to perform in the Folies-Bergère." Raised eyebrows all around. "Never mind," the translator said soothingly. "Herr Reinhardt hopes that another time you'll be free."

FREE.

Birds are free. They can fly where they like. If only I could do the same. Mrs. Caroline had learned about my contract with the Folies and she was furious. First because I hadn't consulted with her, second because she feared they would turn me into a feathered mannequin, preventing me from ever "amounting to anything," and finally because it meant the end of the *Revue Nègre.*

I felt like kicking everyone in sight. Why couldn't people leave me alone? If I stayed in Berlin it would be to study with Herr Reinhardt. But I didn't have much time to think about the future. My days were filled with parties, receptions, journalists who said I "personified Expressionism," whatever *that* meant, faces and more faces, among them a friend of Monsieur Derval's. "I look forward to seeing you in the Folies," he told me. "Don't count on it." "What do you mean?" "I may have changed my mind." "They'll *sue!*" one of the dancers gasped. I shrugged. Lawsuits, contracts—the less I knew about that kind of red tape the better. In St. Louis, we slapped hands to seal a bargain! Anyway, who could make a decision when there was dancing every night and all that wonderful German beer to drink?

A few days later, a Monsieur Lorett visited me in my dressing room. It appeared that Monsieur Derval had sent him. He had three expressions—hurt, angry and charming—which he used alternately. I couldn't *do* this, he insisted. I'd signed a contract and you didn't go back on your word. Poor Monsieur Derval had already hired a number of people because of me. Didn't I realize what the Folies *was?* It took three months to rehearse a show, which involved five hundred people and utilized twelve hundred costumes created by famous designers. They counted on me to be there to inspire the dressmakers and because of me they had built the show around tunes by Spencer Williams and Irving Berlin. . . .

It didn't take long to make up my mind. Herr Reinhardt hadn't mentioned Irving Berlin, whom I adored. Besides, twelve hundred costumes . . . Just as I was about to say yes, I decided to test my worth, since *I* was now introduced in public as the "famous" Josephine. "If you want me to leave Berlin, it will cost you an extra four hundred francs a show." Silence. Monsieur Lorett scurried away—for good, I presumed—but the next day he was back. "Since Monsieur Derval has already invested heavily in the show because of you, he is forced to accept. Please return to Paris at once."

A show, like a love affair, ends in sorrow. During our tearful farewells, we all swore to keep in touch. Sidney was leaving for Moscow with two musician friends. As he kissed me goodbye he murmured, "When I hit my high notes I'll think of you, little bird." "I'll never dance like I did to your clarinet," I replied. "It lifted me right off the ground."

Rainer Maria Rilke

BERLIN LETTER

To Countess Manon zu Solms-Laubach
Hôtel de Russie
Rome, April 11, 1910

This is only to catch up, but still you must know how much I enjoyed your kind letter of January 23. It reached me in Berlin, where (you will remember) I never like being; among the things that come together on such rare visits, there are

---

Rainer Marie Rilke (1875-1926) is widely considered the most important lyric poet of twentieth-century Germany. His Sketches of Malte Laurids Brigge *was panned in Berlin and no doubt contributed to his lifelong disdain for the city.*

always some that are warm, good, yes, quite indispensable: I don't want to complain. But there are always too many then for me (who am adhering more and more to an aloof and solitary life), and Berlin hasn't the way of feeding one things one after the other; one gets everything thrown into one's house at once, one is supposed to see and accomplish everything without coming to one's senses; it is assumed that one has a freshness, an uninterrupted capability, a prompt presence of mind, which I can muster only occasionally and only way inside for my work. So in Berlin I always fare like a bad schoolboy who is behind in everything and ends by no longer grasping from his place of punishment what is going on at the blackboard.

E.T.A. Hoffmann

RITTER GLUCK

USUALLY THERE ARE still several lovely days in the late fall in Berlin. The cheerful sun breaks out of the clouds, and the moisture in the soft breezes that drift through the streets quickly evaporates. A gaudy stream of people wanders along the Lindenstrasse to the Zoological Gardens—dandies, solid citizens with their wives and adored children, all dressed in their Sunday best, clergymen, Jewesses, junior barristers, prostitutes, professors, milliners, dancers, officers, etc. Soon all the tables at Klaus's and at Weber's are occupied; the coffee

E. T. A. Hoffmann's fantastic stories represent the heart of the German Romantic movement. In "Ritter Gluck," Hoffmann (1776-1822) combined his love of music and the magic of the Brothers Grimm with the frenetic enthusiasm of the Romantics.

steams, the dandies light their thin cigars; everyone chats, quarrels about war and peace, about Mademoiselle Beth-mann's shoes, whether they were recently gray or green, about the closed commercial state and the bad pennies, etc., until everything dissolves into an aria from *Fanchon*, in which a harp that is out of tune, a couple of untuned violins, a consumptive flute, and a spastic bassoon torment themselves and the people nearby. Close to the railing that separates the crowd at Weber's from the Heerstrasse are several small round tables and garden chairs. One can breathe fresh air here, observe those coming and going; one is remote from the cacaphonic racket of that execrable orchestra. That is where I sit, abandoning myself to playful reveries in which sympathetic figures appear with whom I chat about learning, art, everything that is supposedly dearest to man. The crowd of strollers weaves past me more and more gayly, but nothing disturbs me, nothing can scatter my imaginary companions. Only the damned trio from an extremely vile waltz drags me from my dream world. I hear only the screeching upper register of the violins and flute and the snoring bass of the bassoon; the sounds rise and fall, keeping firmly to octaves that lacerate the ear, and I cry out involuntarily like a person seized by a burning pain, "What insane music! What abominable octaves!" Someone murmurs next to me, "Accursed fate! Another octave-chaser!"

I looked up and only then became aware that a man had sat down at the same table, his eyes riveted on me; I could not take my eyes off him.

I had never seen a face, a figure, which had made such an impression on me so quickly. A gently curved nose was attached to a wide, open forehead, which had noticeable swellings above the busy, partly gray eyebrows, beneath which eyes blazed forth with an almost youthful fire (the man was probably over fifty). The delicately formed chin was a strange contrast to the closed mouth, and a ludicrous smile produced by the curious play of muscles in his sunken cheeks seemed to rebel against the deep, melancholy seriousness which rested on his forehead. There were only a few gray locks of hair behind his large ears which stuck straight out from his head. A very wide, modern frock coat enveloped his large gaunt frame. Just as my glance met his, he cast down his eyes and continued the occupation that my exclamation had evidently interrupted. With evident satisfaction, he was shaking out some tobacco from various little paper bags into a large tin can that was in front of him and was dampening it with red wine from a quarter liter bottle. The music had stopped; I felt compelled to address him.

"It is a relief that the music has stopped," I said. "It was unendurable."

The old man cast a fleeting glance at me and shook out the last paper bag.

"It would be better not to play at all," I continued. "Isn't that your opinion?"

"I don't have an opinion," he said. "You are a musician and a connoisseur by profession."

"You are mistaken. I am neither. I once learned how to play the piano and the thorough bass, as one must as part of a good education; and at that time I was told, among other things, that nothing produced a more unpleasant effect than having the bass pace the soprano in octave intervals. I accepted that at the time as authoritative and I have since found it always verified."

"Really?" he interrupted me, as he stood up and strode slowly and thoughtfully towards the musicians while frequently striking his forehead with the flat of his hand, his face upturned, like someone trying to awaken a recollection. I saw him speaking to the musicians whom he had treated with lordly dignity. He returned and had scarcely sat down when they began to play the overture to *Iphigenia in Aulis.*

With half-closed eyes, his folded arms resting on the table, he listened to the *andante.* Tapping his left foot gently, he signaled the entrance of the voices; then he raised his head—quickly casting a glance around—he rested his left hand with fingers spread apart on the table as if he were playing a chord on a piano, and he raised his right hand up. He was the Kapellmeister signalling the orchestra the start of a new tempo—his right hand dropped and the *allegro* began! A burning glow flushed his pale cheeks; his eyebrows met on his wrinkled forehead; an inner storm inflamed his wild expression with a fire that increasingly consumed the smile that still hovered around his half-opened mouth. Then he leaned back and raised his eyebrows; the play of muscles around his mouth began again; his eyes shone; a deep inner pain was released in a voluptuous pleasure that convulsively shook his inner being. He drew a breath from deep within his lungs; drops formed on his forehead; he signalled for the entrance of the *tutti* and other major places; his right hand kept the beat, and with his left he pulled out a handkerchief and wiped his face. Thus he clothed with flesh and color the skeleton of the overture played by the pair of violins. I heard the soft, melting elegy which the flute utters when the storm of the violins and the bass viols has exhausted itself and the thunder of the drums is silent; I heard the softly played tones of the cello and the bassoon which filled the heart with ineffable sadness; the *tutti* returned, the *unisono* strode on like a sublime and lofty giant, the somber lament die away under his crushing tread.

The overture was over; he let his arms fall, and he saw there with his eyes closed like a person exhausted by excessive exertion. His bottle was empty; I filled his glass with Burgundy, which I had meanwhile ordered. He sighed deeply and seemed to be awaking from a dream. I urged him to drink, which he did without ceremony, and while he dashed off the glass in one swallow, he cried, "I am satisfied with the performance! The orchestra performed very nicely!"

"And yet," I interrupted, "and yet, only the pale outline of a masterpiece that has been composed with vivid colors was presented."

"Do I judge rightly? You are not a Berliner!"

"Quite right. I only stay here from time to time."

"The Burgundy is good. But it is getting cold here."

"Let's go inside and finish the bottle."

"A good suggestions. I don't know you; but on the other hand, you don't know me either. We will not ask each other's names; names are sometimes a nuisance. I will drink the Burgundy; it cost me nothing and we are comfortable together and that is enough."

He said all this with a good-natured cordiality. We had entered the room. When he sat down, he opened his frock coat and I noticed with surprise that he was wearing under it an embroidered waistcoat, long coattails, black velvet britches, and a quite small dagger. He buttoned the coat again carefully.

"Why did you ask me if I was a Berliner?" I began.

"Because in that case I would have been obliged to leave you."

"That sounds mysterious."

"Not in the least, as soon as I tell you that I—well, that I am a composer."

"I still can't guess what you mean."

"Then forgive my remark, for I see you do not understand anything about Berlin and Berliners."

He rose and paced violently up and down a few times; then he stepped to the window and scarcely audibly sang the chorus of the priestess from *Iphigenia in Tauris,* while tapping on the windowpane from time to time at the entrance of the *tutti* passage. With astonishment I noticed that he gave certain different directions to the melody that were striking in their power and novelty. I let him go on. He finished and returned to his seat. Quite taken by the man's strange behavior and extraordinary signs of a rare musical talent, I remained silent. After a while he began.

"Have you never composed?"

"Yes, I have tried my skill; only I found that everything which I had written in moments of inspiration afterwards seemed to be flat and boring. So I gave it up."

"You acted wrongly. The very fact that you rejected your own attempts is no bad sign of your talent. One learns music as a boy because father and mother wish it. So one fiddles and bangs away; but without noticing it, one's senses become more receptive to melody. Perhaps it was the half-forgotten theme of a little song which one now sang differently, the first thought of one's own; and this embryo, laboriously nourished by strange powers, grew to be a giant which consumed everything around and was transformed into your blood and marrow. Ah—how to suggest the thousand ways by which one can come to composing! It is a wide highway: everyone romps around on it and exults and shouts, 'We are the sacred people! We have attained the goal!' One enters the kingdom of dreams through the ivory gate: only a few even see the gate, even fewer pass through! It looks strange here. Absurd figures hover here and there, but they have character—one more than the other. They cannot be seen on the highway; they can only be found behind the ivory gate. It is difficult to get out of this kingdom; monsters block the way as they do in front of Alzinen's castle—everything spins, turns—many dream away the dream in the kingdom of dreams—they dissolve in dreams—they do not cast a shadow any longer, for otherwise, by the shadow, they would know about the ray of light that passes through this kingdom; but only a few, awakened from the dream, arise and stride through the kingdom of dreams—they attain the truth—the highest moment is there: contact with the eternal, the ineffable! Look at the sun; it is the triad from which the chords, like stars, shoot out and entwine you with threads of fire. You lie as in a cocoon of fire until the soul swings up to the sun."

He jumped up at the last words, cast his eyes upward and raised his hand. Then he sat down again and quickly emptied his refilled glass. A silence arose which I did not want to break for fear of getting the extraordinary man off the track. Finally he continued more calmly.

"When I was in the kingdom of dreams, a thousand aches and worries tortured me. It was night and I was terrified by the grinning larvae of the monsters who dashed out at me and sometimes dragged me into the ocean's abyss, sometimes carried me high into the sky. Rays of light shot through the night and these rays of light were tones which encircles me with delightful clarity. I awoke from my pains and saw a large, bright eye that was looking into an organ; and as it looked, tones sounded forth and shimmered and entwined themselves in marvelous chords that had never before been conceived. Melodies streamed back and forth, and I swam in this stream and was about to drown. Then the eye looked at me and sustained me above the roaring waves. It became night again; two colossi in gleaming armor strode towards me: the Tonic and the Dominant. They snatched me up, but the eye said smiling, 'I know what fills your heart with yearning. The gentle, soft youth Tierce will walk among the colossi; you will hear his sweet voice; you will see me again and my melodies will be yours.'"

He stopped.

"And you saw the eye again?"

"Yes, I saw it again. For many years I sighed in the kingdom of dreams there—indeed, there—I sat in a marvelous valley and listened to the flowers singing together. Only a sunflower was silent and sadly bowed her closed calyx to the ground. Invisible bonds drew me to her—she raised her head—the calyx opened and shone toward me from within the eye. Now tones, like rays of light, flowed from my head to the flowers, which greedily drank them. The leaves of the sunflower grew bigger and bigger—fire streamed from them encompassed me—the eye had vanished and I was in the calyx."

With the last words he sprang up and hurried out of the room with a quick, youthful stride. I awaited his return in vain; I decided, therefore, to go back to the city.

When I was near the Brandenburg Gate, I saw a lanky figure striding along in the darkness and immediately recognized my odd friend. I spoke to him.

"Why did you leave me so quickly?"

"It got too hot and euphony began to sound."

"I don't understand you!"

"All the better."

"All the worse, for I would like to understand you completely."

"Don't you hear anything?"

"No."

"It is gone! Let us go. Usually I don't like company, but—you do not compose—you are not a Berliner."

"I cannot fathom why you are so prejudiced against Berliners. Here, where art is respected and practiced widely, I would think a man with your artistic soul would feel happy."

"You are mistaken! I am damned to wander here as my torment in barren space, like a departed spirit."

"In barren space, here, in Berlin?"

"Yes, it is barren around me, for no kindred spirit joins me. I am alone."

"But the artists! The composers!"

"Away with them! They carp and niggle—refine everything to the smallest measure; rake through everything just to find one wretched thought. From chattering so much about art and artistic sensitivity and what have you—they never get around to creating, and if they do happen to feel as if they had to bring a few wretched thoughts to light, the fearful coldness reveals their great distance from the sun—it is Laplandish work."

"Your criticism seems much too harsh to me. At least the splendid productions in the theater must satisfy you."

"Once I prevailed upon myself to go to the theater to hear the opera of my young friend—what is it called? Oh, the whole world is in this opera! The spirits of hell stride through the bright crowd of elegant people—everything in it has a voice and an all-powerful sound—the devil, I mean *Don Juan!* But I couldn't last through the overture, which was spewed forth *prestissimo,* without meaning or understanding; and I had prepared myself for it with fasting and prayer because I know that euphony is much too moved by these masses and has an impure appeal.

"Even if I have to admit that Mozart's masterpieces are mostly neglected here in a way scarcely explicable, still Gluck's work certainly enjoys a dignified performance."

"You think so? I wanted to hear *Iphigenia in Tauris* once. As I entered the theater, I heard how the overture of *Iphigenia in Tauris* was being played. Hm—I think, a mistake. *This Iphigenia* is being given! I am astonished when the *andante* with which Iphigenia is received in Tauris begins and the storm follows. Twenty years lie in between! The whole effect, the tragedy's whole well-planned exposition is lost. A quiet set—a storm—the Greeks are cast on land, the opera is there! Well, do you think the composer tossed out the overture so that one can blow it how and where one wants to, like a little trumpet piece?"

"I admit the blunder. Still, everything is done to promote Gluck's works."

"Oh, yes indeed!" he said curtly and then smiled bitterly and ever more bitterly. Suddenly he rose, and nothing could stay him. He vanished in a moment, and for several days I sought him in vain in the Zoological Gardens.

SEVERAL MONTHS HAD passed. One cold rainy night I was delayed in a remote section of the city and was hurrying to my home in the Friedrichstrasse. I had to pass the theater.

The sound of music, of trumpets and drums, reminded me that Gluck's *Armida* was being performed, and I was on the point of going in when a strange soliloquy by the windows, where almost every tone of the orchestra could be heard, aroused my attention.

"Now the king is coming—they are playing the March—Drum away! Just drum away! That's very gay! Yes they have to do it eleven times today—otherwise the parade isn't enough of a parade. Ah Ha!—*maestoso*—poke along, boys. Look, there's a super with a shoelace dragging. Right, for the twelfth time and always striking the dominant. O ye eternal powers! It is never going to end! Now he is making a bow—Armida very humbly acknowledges the applause. Once again? Right. Two soldiers are still missing. Now they are banging into the recitative. What evil spirit holds me here in his spell?"

"The spell is dissolved." I cried. "Come along!"

I quickly seized my odd friend from the Zoological Gardens for the soliloquist was none other—by the arm and dragged him off with me. He seemed surprised and followed me in silence. We had already reached the Friedrichstrasse when he suddenly stopped.

"I know you," said he. "You were in the Zoological Gardens. We did a lot of talking. I drank wine—and became heated—afterwards euphony rang for two days. I endured a great deal—it is past!"

"I am delighted that chance has led me to you again. Let us become better acquainted with one another. I don't live very far from here. How would it be—"

"I cannot and may not go to another's house."

"No. You won't escape me. I will come to you."

"Then you will still have to walk a few hundred steps with me. But didn't you want to go to the theater?"

"I wanted to hear *Armida*, but now—"

"You shall hear *Armida* right *now!* Come along!"

We walked along the Friedrichstrasse in silence; he suddenly turned into a cross-street, and I was scarcely able to follow him, because he ran down the street so quickly until he finally stopped in front of a modest house. He knocked for rather a long time before the door was finally opened. Feeling

our way in the dark, we found the stairs and then a room in
the upper floor, the door of which my guide carefully locked
behind us. I heard another door being opened. Soon he came
back with a light, and the appearance of the strangely furnished room surprised me not a little. Chairs ornamented with
an old-fashioned richness, a wall clock with a gilded case, and
a broad, cumbersome mirror gave everything the gloomy
appearance of a past splendor. In the middle stood a small
piano on which were a porcelain inkstand and several sheets of
paper lined for music. A closer glance at these materials convinced me, however, that nothing had been written for a long
time, for the paper was quite yellowed, and thick spiderwebs
covered the inkstand. The man stepped over to a cupboard in
the corner of the room which I had not noticed before, and
when he pulled aside the curtain, I saw a row of beautifully
bound books with golden letters: *Orfeo, Armida, Alceste, Iphigenia,*
etc., in brief, I saw Gluck's masterpieces standing together.

"You have Gluck's complete works?" I cried.

He did not answer; but his mouth twisted in a con-
vulsive smile, and in a flash the play of muscles in his sunken

cheeks distorted his face to a fearful mask. His somber glance directed fixedly at me, he seized one of the books—it was *Armida*—and strode solemnly toward the piano. I opened it quickly and set up the music stand. He seemed pleased with that. He opened the book and—who can describe my astonishment—I saw music paper, but without a single note written on it.

He said, "Now I will play the overture. Turn the pages at the right moments!" I promised to do so; then he played marvelously and masterfully, with complete chords, the majestic *tempo di marcia* with which the overture begins, almost completely true to the original. The *allegro*, however, merely had Gluck's main thoughts woven into it. He introduced so many new and inspired twists that my astonishment grew and grew. His modulations were especially striking without becoming harsh, and he knew how to add so many melodic *melismas* that they seemed to be recurring in ever-rejuvenated form. His face glowed, sometimes his eyebrows were drawn together and a long restrained anger seemed about to burst forth; sometimes his eyes swam in tears of deepest melancholy. At times he sang the theme with a pleasant tenor voice while both hands were working at artistic *melismas.* Then, in a quite special way, he knew how to imitate the hollow sound of the drum. I turned the pages industriously by watching his glance. The overture was over and he fell back in his chair exhausted, his eyes closed. But soon he leaned forward again and said in a hollow voice, while hastily turning more empty pages of the book, "I wrote all this, my good sir, when I came from the kingdom of dreams. But I betrayed that which is holy to the unholy and an ice cold hand reached into my glowing heart! It did not break. Then I was damned to wander among the unholy like a departed spirit—formless, so that no one would recognize me until the sunflower should raise me again to the eternal. Ah— now let us sing Armida's scene!"

Then he sang the final scene of *Armida* with an expression that penetrated my soul. Here too he deviated noticeably from the true original; but the transformed music was the Gluck scene in a higher power. He recapitulated powerfully in sound, and in the highest measure, everything that hate, love, despair, madness can express. His voice seemed to be that of a young man, for it swelled up from the deepest groan to a penetrating power. All my fibers trembled. I was beside myself. When he had finished, I hurled myself into his arms and cried in a strained voice. "What is it? Who are you?"

He stood up and measured me with an earnest, penetrating glance; but when I wanted to ask more, he had vanished with the light through the door and left me in the darkness. Almost a quarter of an hour passed; I had despaired of ever seeing him again and was seeking to open the door, oriented by the position of the piano, when he suddenly returned in an embroidered court dress, with a rich waistcoat, his dagger at his side and the light in his hand.

I was paralyzed. Solemnly he strode towards me, seized me gently by the hand, and said, smiling strangely, "*I am Ritter Gluck!*"

Christa Wolf

THE QUEST FOR CHRISTA T.

HE FIRST SAW her at lunchtime in the commons, when she was still a student. He'd come from another university to attend a conference which still had two more days to run. She's standing in line—who is she, where have I seen her before? That's how it began, at least on one side. He remembers the picture on the wall in his parents' living room, the girl seen in profile, that's who she is, the picture cut from a calendar, portrait of an Egyptian queen.

Christa Wolf is the author of numerous novels set in East Berlin, including Cassandra, No Place on Earth, *and her 1970 masterwork,* The Quest for Christa T., *from which this excerpt is taken. Today she lives in Berlin.*

He asks a mutual friend to take him to her table, and he invites her to the party at the end of the conference tomorrow evening. She, neither surprised nor offended, simply accepts; no difficulty at all. Except that he cannot, unfortunately, persuade himself that she's particularly interested, likewise the next evening, and the day following the party, when they walk by the canal. Then he has to leave, and he knows: I've made no progress whatever. Although he's never wanted anything more in his life.

Later that must have turned the scales.

It was a long time before we saw him; but we knew from Christa T. herself that someone was in the offing. He's wanted me for a long time.

Then she looked innocently into our inquisitive faces. That was all.

So we'd better take a few steps back.

How young she is! And how she longs to have passionate feelings! Everything she sees is fresh and new, every face, every movement, the whole city, she won't allow anything to be remote or strange, she lives in the present, bewitched by colors, smells, sounds: *Always to be making new connections, always to be moving on from them . . .* The city belongs to her—will she ever be so rich again? The child is hers, sitting forlornly in the corner of a streetcar and asking his mother about everything he can hear outside but not see; the man with black hair—*a lot of white in his narrowed eyes, and a hard trait in his features,* to whom she entrusts tenderness, she feels hot all over when she looks at him, he smiles and says *Auf Wiedersehen* when he leaves. The young gardener from whom she buys the far too expensive lilac and whom she bedazzles: I can't resist such a handsome young man . . . But she gives the lilac to a perplexed husband who comes rushing out of a meeting because he's remembered it's his wedding anniversary and now all the flower shops are closed. And even the lady who comes to visit her son belongs to her, a theology student, Christa T. sizes him up, intelligent but proud: no friend of ours—but then he belongs to her as well.

All this was preparation for her love, for that's what this chapter is about. She sends friendly answers to Justus's letters; then at the right moment his letters stop coming. He had the gift of doing the right thing at the right moment. She liked that. Meanwhile, she didn't lose his telephone number; but it's unlikely she gave it more than a glance or two. One couldn't force her, she couldn't force herself; nothing happened to her quickly, but much had happened already, so now she felt more frequently where it was leading, but this feeling was at once mixed, as was usual for her, with despair: *Suddenly she was seized by a great fear that she couldn't write, wouldn't be able to put into words the feelings that filled her.* In which case it's safer to talk of a third person, whether it's oneself or someone else whom one is calling, for example, "she." One can perhaps slip more easily away from that third person, one doesn't have to be drawn into the *misfortune of her false life,* one can place her side by side with oneself, observe her thoroughly, as one customarily observes other people.

All this could become love, but the decision still has to be taken. One day, when she's once more running across the road, with a crowd of people surging toward her at the intersection, all single people, but every one of them a stranger to her—suddenly she stops, and shudders: Aren't I pretending to myself? How long can one go on waiting? Have I still really got the time? And who precisely does belong to me?

Within an hour she has called the number which, as may be seen, she has been carrying about with her.—So it's you, says Justus, I might have thought it.—That he was tired of waiting, that he was beginning to have doubts and had already been tempted to inquire about her—of all this not a word.

When? he says instead.

That's the right beginning for something that's going to last.

But I can't promise, she tells herself, as she walks from the telephone booth, of course I can't promise anything.

While writing this—in all good conscience, because every statement is doubly authenticated and stands up to the scrutiny of review—while leafing further through the reddish-brown Berlin notebook and coming upon the line "Justus, dear beloved Justus!", while endeavoring to create the room in which their first meeting can occur—while all this is going on an old mistrustfulness overcomes me again, though I thought I had quelled it, I wouldn't have expected it to return at this of all moments. Mightn't the net that has been woven and set for her finally turn out to be incapable of catching her? The sentences I have written, yes. Also the ways she traveled, a room she has lived in, a landscape near and dear to her, a house, even a feeling—but not herself. For she's hard to catch. Even if I could do it, faithfully present everything about her that I've known or experienced, even then its conceivable that the person to whom I tell the story, whom I need and whose support I solicit, might finally know nothing about her.

As good as nothing.

Unless I can contrive to say the most important thing about her, which is this: Christa T. had a vision of herself. I can't prove this in the way that I could prove she lived here or there, at this time or that, and that she read this book or that from the university library. But the books are neither here nor there, I haven't looked up her old library cards; if the worst came to the worst, I'd simply invent a few titles. No, one doesn't invent a person's visions, though one does sometimes find them. I've known of her vision for a long time: since that moment twelve years before, when I saw her blowing a trumpet.

For we're now in the year 1955.

It's a long time before we see Justus, as I've said; he was withheld from us. And besides, we were wondering: a vet's wife in Mecklenburg, was that to be it? For one is always involuntarily grasping for definitions. But then came the fancy-dress ball, at which Christa T. arrived as Sophie La Roche, though she hadn't dressed up at all, she wore only her goldish-brown dress with the exotic pattern, telling everyone who she was supposed to be. Justus beside her, no more dressed up than she herself, was playing the part of Lord Seymour, at least that's what he said. Nobody knew whether this idea was exceptionally lofty or simply contrary; but in any case we could at last take a look at Justus, and in doing so we found that we could quietly drop all the definitions.

It was, I suppose, what people call a party, one of the first, and we weren't at all sure how things are done at parties. Yet when we looked at our hosts we felt that a party was what it had to be: as people arrived they were told to do as they pleased, *vorurteilsfrei*—don't be afraid! and Christa T. nodded sensibly, looked around in the two dimly lit rooms, plucked a few paper streamers from the rubber plant and draped them around her shoulders, emptied a package of confetti over Justus's head, and said: This place is all right.

I can't say I shared her feeling. I felt she'd planned something special for this evening and it couldn't be properly accommodated in this society where all the costumes looked provocative and yet so repressed. Her plan seemed to be aimed against Justus himself, or at him. I didn't know what to do. I even wanted to warn him, side with him, I liked him. Then I saw that he didn't need any warnings. He kept quite cool, for his time of uncertainty had passed long ago.

And hers? Or was it she who was mutely asking for some kind of support?—Mademoiselle La Roche, I said, when nobody could hear us, you don't seem to realize what you're taking upon yourself: the fate of La Roche! An over-ardent and rather sentimental dreamer, chained to a life in the country against her will, so that she pours all her ungratified longing into an invented character . . .

Much worse than that, Christa T. replied. If it was La Roche, things wouldn't be so bad. But it's that character who's meant, Fräulein von Sternheim herself: and her fate.

You're joking, I said.

Justus brought some champagne and stood there beside us. But I could go on talking.

Seduction? Intrigues? A false marriage with this rogue Derby? A mournful country life in the English provinces? And, for God's sake, virtue?!

Precisely that, said Christa T. And finally her reward for everything: Lord Seymour, the paragon!

Mademoiselle, said Justus, you shouldn't call me that.

We'll see what you'll be called, Christa T. said.

She drank off her champagne in one gulp, looking at him. His smile was hopeful, but not self-confident.

It was working out, it really could work out.

I thought I could now see her plan more clearly. She had found a way to show him what she'd be giving up if she went along with him. She seemed to have just realized this herself, and she was scared again, it was a crucial moment. But Justus, whether he knew it or not, did the right thing: he behaved as if he'd known this long before she did, as if this was precisely the vital point, as if there was no question of giving anything up. And he was telling her so, without wasting a word, simply by the way he raised his glass to her, took her glass from her hand, and led her away to dance. Since, as he saw, her decision had been made, it was up to him to make the last step easy for her: there was to be no last step, only one step among many others.

She was grateful to him for the certainty he gave her, and with good reason. Then he let her dance for as long as she liked and with whomever she liked, didn't dance himself, didn't drink much, waited until he could say: Let's go.—Then she left her partner standing and went at once. She waved to me airily and left us, and those of us who stayed behind might well ask ourselves why we'd ever doubted that she'd get married in a simple happy way.

That evening she wanted to take herself and us a few steps back, one or two centuries back, so as to see ourselves more clearly. In a hundred years, no, in fifty, we too shall be historical figures standing on a stage. Why wait so long? Why, since after all it's inevitable, why not take a few strides and jump on the stage oneself, try out a few of the roles, before

one defines oneself, rejecting this one or that as too tall an
order, finding others already occupied and feeling secretly envi-
ous of their occupants: but finally to accept one role in which
everything depends on how you play it, depends, thus on you
and you alone. Hers: the wife of a man who'll be a veterinary
surgeon and who knows that she not only sought him out but
created him especially, and that each must compel the other to
live to the full extent of their powers, if they are never to lose
one another again.

That evening he took her home with him. I've given
up the idea of inventing the room, it's not important. And now
she doesn't need time any more. The playing was over, the role
lapsed into irrelevancy, he loved her.

Acknowledgments

Excerpt from *Speak, Memory* by Vladimir Nabokov ©1989 by the Estate of Vladimir Nabokov. Reprinted by permission of Vintage Books, a Division of Random House, Inc.

"The Job" from *Collected Short Stories* by Bertolt Brecht. Published by Methuen London. © Suhrkamp Verlag, Frankfurt am Main 1967. Translation ©1983 by Stefan S. Brecht. Reprinted by permission of Reed Books.

Excerpt from *The Berlin Diaries 1940-1945* by Marie Vassiltchikov ©1985 by the Estate of Marie Harnden. Reprinted by permission of Alfred A. Knopf, Inc.

Excerpt from *Berlin Alexanderplatz* by Alfred Döblin ©1983 by Walter Verlag AG, Olten. Reprinted by permission of The Continuum Publishing Company of New York.

Excerpt from *Gravity's Rainbow* by Thomas Pynchon ©1973 by Thomas Pynchon. Reprinted by permission of Viking Penguin, a division of Penguin Books USA, Inc.

"Picture Postcard, Berlin" from *Franz Kafka: Letters to Friends, Family, and Editors* by Franz Kafka, translated by Richard and Clara Winston ©1958, 1977 by Schocken Books Inc. Reprinted by permission of Schocken Books, published by Pantheon Books, a division of Random House, Inc.

The song *The Lavendar Lay* by Marcellus Schiffer, translated by Laurence Senelick. English translation reprinted with permission of Laurence Senelick.

"The Party at the Wall" by Bennett Owen from the *National Review*, December 22, 1989. Reprinted by permission of the *National Review.*

Excerpt from *Pentimento* by Lillian Hellman ©1973 by Lillian Hellman. Reprinted by permission of Little, Brown and Company.

"A Berlin Diary" from *Goodbye to Berlin* by Christopher Isherwood ©1935 by Christopher Isherwood. Reprinted by permission of New Directions Publishing Corp.

"Berlin" from *Josephine* by Josephine Baker and Jo Bouillon and translated by Mariana Fitzpatrick. English translation ©1977 by Harper & Row, Publishers, Inc. Reprinted by permission of HarperCollins Publishers, Inc.

Excerpt from *The Letters of Rainer Maria Rilke* by Rainer Maria Rilke ©1945 by W. W. Norton & Company, Inc., renewed ©1972 by M. D. Herter Norton. Translated from the German by Jane Bannard Greene and M. D. Herter Norton. Reprinted by permission of W. W. Norton & Company, Inc.